C L

FOLK
TALES

CLARE
FOLK
TALES

RUTH MARSHALL

The
History
Press
Ireland

To the wise women and the heroes.
To Carolanne, Iain and Rosie Bloom.

First published 2013

The History Press Ireland
50 City Quay
Dublin 2
Ireland
www.thehistorypress.ie

British Library Cataloguing in Publication Data.
A catalogue record for this book is available from the British Library.

ISBN 978 1 84588 761 2

Typesetting and origination by The History Press
Printed by TJ International Ltd, Padstow, Cornwall.

CONTENTS

ACKNOWLEDGEMENTS

Thank you to all who told me stories as I hitched around County Clare many years ago; to the kind gentlemen of the Local Studies Centre in Ennis; to the children and teachers of the 1930s who collected stories for the Schools Folklore Scheme (1937-38); to Criostoir Mac Carthaigh, archivist, Irish Folklore Commission, UCD.

Thank you to Iain Symes-Marshall, Carolanne Lamont and Susie Minto for long conversations of encouragement and support. I couldn't have done it without you.

INTRODUCTION

I first came to East Clare as a naive 'blow-in' in 1986. I couldn't drive then and if I wanted to get anywhere I had to hitch lifts. When you are hitching, people tell you stories and ask for your story, because that's what you do to shorten the road. Back then I wasn't too sure what my story was, but thankfully it's a bit clearer now. Now I know that wherever you are there is a story to hear, whether that's in a small shop-come-pub in someone's front room, the elderly neighbour who drops in of an evening, or the stranger who happens to be walking on the same stretch of otherwise deserted shore. Stories seep into your cells and become part of you until sometime later you realise you know that story, and tell it again.

That's how it was with some of these stories, but with others I spent days in front of the ancient microfiche machines in the Local Studies Centre in Ennis searching through reels of film of handwritten jotters full of folklore collected by schoolchildren in the 1930s. These stores of collective wisdom are part of the archives of the Irish Folklore Commission and they are a wee seam of pure gold. The only problem is that there is so much interesting material there it was hard to stick to looking for stories and not to go off on tangents of skipping games or cures for whooping cough.

One of the first snippets of story I found there was about a woman called Biddy Collins who lived in a cabin on a bog near Tulla, and who was regularly visited by fairies who told her stories in the night. In a way, that is how I felt as I worked on this book. Each day I got on with the stuff of living: all the necessary chopping of wood, carrying of water, feeding the cat, etc. At night, the fairies and other characters from the stories in this book came to visit me, retold their tales, and helped me to be comfortable in using my own voice, with its distinctly Scottish accent, to tell these stories from County Clare.

It seemed to me that in undertaking this project I needed to be aligned with the fairy presences of this place where I have made my home. I am used to working with landscape and through observing the elements (earth, water, air, fire) coming to meet the spirit of place. I am used to that '*genius loci*' sharing its story with me, speaking through me. Working on this book required a different approach: the stories exist already. They have emerged over hundreds, perhaps thousands of years, spoken into the sleeping ears of those who lived here in County Clare. I did not need to dig deep into the earth to find these stories. I had only to mine the rich seam of memory – my own and those recorded many years ago.

I attempted to attune as closely as I could to the very essence of the tales. To put myself into the geographic locations, to feel in my body the living stories, and to re-tell them from that embodied place: from the inside out. I tried to be as true to the stories as possible. I asked for and genuinely felt the support of the mysterious otherworld. The work, both researching and writing my re-tellings, has been a joy and a gift. I have felt carried, supported, and encouraged by the stories themselves.

The stories I have included will not be everybody's choice of typical Clare folk tales, but they are the ones that speak to me, that grabbed my attention and demanded to be told. They are stories that I am happy to tell, that sit well on me, that contain some essential truth that still has relevance for us.

I am conscious that the largest section is on Wise Women, Wild Women, Harridans & Hags, and I make no apology for this. These are the stories that I found most interesting and exciting. I found myself empathising with the hags, who were often maligned in the old tales, as a patriarchal society belittles women and presents them as wicked for simply being wilful. I found that when I pieced together snippets of the same story from different places, I found the 'back story' that explained, for example, how the Cailleach Bealaha was wronged as a young woman, and thus became a vindictive 'hag' in later life. Stories explain how we have come to be as we are. Even hags had hearts that were broken.

I come back to the old woman Biddy Collins. Some may have thought her mad or deluded, but I saw in this brief glimpse of her, a woman who knew the power of story and the power of blessing. I hope you will find this book holds something similar that might enrich your life. So I'd like to offer you the blessing she spoke when she told her stories. To you, readers, listeners, tellers, re-tellers, and to the land of County Clare itself: 'God bless the hearers and tellers, and when 'tis told and those that's telling it.'

Ruth Marshall, 2013

1

WISE WOMEN, WILD WOMEN, HARRIDANS & HAGS

BIDDY EARLY

The first stories I heard when I moved from the north of Scotland to East Clare in 1986 were about Biddy Early. Biddy was not a mythical character, but a real flesh and blood woman who lived in East Clare and died at a good age in around 1874. The stories spoke of her as a healer, a wise woman who knew about herbs. They said she had a blue bottle through which she could tell the future. Biddy, they said, was a red-headed independent woman who had had at least four husbands, the last of these being a man of thirty when she herself was in her seventies. With her cottage door always open, Biddy was loved by the common people for her cures, and yet feared and resented by others, including certain priests, who labelled her a witch.

As Biddy's cottage at Kilbarron near Feakle was only a few miles from where I lived, I felt I must pay a visit, and set out on the quiet road to hitch a lift. One man told me that when he had gone to pay his respects at Biddy's old home, he was met at the gate with a sudden clap of thunder and a flash of lightning, and so had run off in fright! So it was with trepidation that I walked up the muddy track to the tumbled-down cottage. Would I be welcome here? A little nervously I stopped at the doorway to ask permission to enter. Just then a little wren flew in through the ruined window and crossed the room towards me. That was greeting enough for me. The wren somehow to me is always female, just as the robin is always male. I felt myself welcomed by that humble little brown bird: a plain and simple wee bird with no pretensions. I thought then that that is what healing is: nothing fancy, no big deal, just simple everyday magic. Biddy and a little brown birdie welcomed me in, and it felt like a blessing.

I had heard the story of how 'Doctor Bill' (Loughnane) had suffered terrible misfortune after doing up the cottage in the 1960s and trying to make a commercial venture of it. Biddy, after all, had never charged for her services, but had gratefully received whatever people brought to her. And they brought what they could: fresh baked bread, eggs, poitín.

Biddy Early's cottage was up for sale again recently, once more with the hope that someone would take it and turn it into a tourist attraction. It makes me wonder, why would a little brown bird want to be dressed up like a parrot and displayed? I think that anyone who really wants to meet Biddy Early does so. I believe that the spirit of Biddy Early is still among us in the simple, humble workings of those who heal and bless.

So, that is my story of meeting Biddy Early in the 1980s. Now here are some of the older stories told about her …

As well as knowing the uses of herbs, Biddy also had a magic blue bottle that she would look into to see if a person would respond to her cure or not. People say that the manner in which Biddy acquired this bottle was somewhat unusual.

Biddy Early had a grown-up son called Paddy. He was a great dancer and he loved hurling. He was coming home late from a dance one night when a party of small men (fairies or 'good people') called to him to come and make up their numbers for a hurling match. Paddy went with them and joined their side. The game was played fast and fierce all through the night, and at last, with Paddy's help, his team won. The players were grateful and showed this by giving Paddy a blue bottle. They said he should give the bottle to his mother, that she would know what to do with it and that it would provide her with a good livelihood. Paddy stuffed the bottle inside his shirt and thanked the men, who vanished suddenly as the cock crowed with the first rays of the sun. When he reached home, Paddy told his story and gave the bottle to Biddy, who went on to do great work with that famous blue bottle!

Once a poor man tried to steal Biddy Early's blue bottle, thinking he could make his fortune with it. He got into Biddy's house when she was not at home, because her door was always open to whoever needed her, but he did not see the bottle anywhere. He was just about to start rifling through Biddy's meagre possessions when his feet suddenly became stuck to the ground. He was very scared then, sure that Biddy knew exactly what he was about. He wished he'd never gone into her house, and he wanted nothing more than to run away before she could catch him there, but he could not lift either foot. He was still fastened there when Biddy came home. She laughed at the sight of him stuck to her floor, then she spoke a few words and his feet came unstuck again. That man never did a day's good after that.

There was a Mrs Murphy who lived around Maghera, near Tulla. One day her daughter began to complain of a pain in her right leg. When this pain had lasted for several days, the doctor came to see the girl, and gave her a bottle of lotion to rub into the sore part of her leg. The lotion made no difference. The girl was still in pain, and she hobbled about with a pronounced limp.

Some of the neighbours suggested that Mrs Murphy should go to see Biddy Early and ask her for a bottle that would cure the girl's condition. They told her stories of how Biddy had helped one man when his cattle were sick, and another when his son was unable to rise from his bed in the morning. Others spoke badly of Biddy Early, saying that she was a witch, and advised Mrs Murphy to have nothing to do with her. Amongst those who spoke against Biddy was one Mr O'Keefe, a close neighbour.

The girl's pain and discomfort worsened and Mrs Murphy finally decided she would go and ask Biddy for help. She rose early in the morning and left the house before anyone could see her, for she wanted no one to know her business. She walked to Feakle and made her way to Biddy Early's cottage.

Biddy was waiting for her at the door and greeted her warmly. There was no need to tell her who she was, nor what she was there for, for Biddy greeted her with, 'So Mrs Murphy, you have come looking for a cure for your daughter's sore leg, have ye?'

Biddy told her where she had come from, described what she had passed on the road there, and mentioned the conversation in Mrs Murphy's kitchen when Mr O'Keefe had tried to scare her off from going to Biddy.

'Ah now,' said Biddy, 'it will not be long before he will need my help himself, but will he dare to ask for it?' As it turned out, a short while afterwards Mr O'Keefe was driving a horse and cart towards Tulla, when the horse shied at Maghera Cross. A terrific wind arose and Mr O'Keefe was blown off his cart into the road and lay there quite senseless until he was found by a passer-by. Mr O'Keefe's own son had to plead with Biddy for her help. With some reluctance she gave him a bottle that cured Mr O'Keefe. As you can imagine, he did not speak ill of Biddy and her cures again.

Anyway, Biddy prepared a bottle for Mrs Murphy's daughter. She took a look through her own blue bottle and saw that the girl would do well if she took the remedy. Mrs Murphy thanked Biddy, and set off on the road home. The road home would take her through the village of Tulla, where there happened to be a fair that day. Despite the busyness of the fair, Mrs Murphy saw no one she recognised as she passed through the streets, which was odd, as she was quite familiar with most of the Tulla people. Nobody spoke to her as she walked through the village, and she saw no cattle there, despite the fair.

Mrs Murphy believed this strange happening was down to Biddy's magic. After all, she had told Biddy that her visit was secret and that she wished it to remain so.

As she drew near to her home, a strange dog viciously attacked Mrs Murphy. It was all she could do to keep hold of the bottle and prevent it from smashing. She chased off the ferocious dog, reached the house with the bottle intact, and gave her daughter the contents. Within a day or two the girl recovered and her leg was good as new.

It was not just the local people around Feakle and East Clare who visited Biddy. Her name was known throughout the county, and people travelled from the furthest corners of West Clare to ask for a cure.

There was a woman who lived in Lissycasy who became ill. Her husband was sceptical about Biddy and her bottle, and told his wife, 'It is all nonsense, I don't believe in Biddy Early or her cures, but to please you, I will go and ask her help. What harm can it do?'

It was a long way to travel, and he was tired when he reached Biddy's cottage. Biddy met him at the door and said, 'So, why did you come all the way from Lissycasey to me looking for a cure, when I know you told your wife you have no faith in it at all?'

The man was amazed and a little shamefaced. Biddy gave him a bottle for his wife anyway and warned him to be careful not to drop it when he would reach a certain spot on his road home. When he reached that place, he was mysteriously pulled from his horse and the bottle broke when it fell to the ground. He returned to Biddy's cottage.

Once again, before he could tell her what had happened, she told him what she had seen. Then she gave him another bottle and warned him again. He was pulled from his horse a second time at that same spot, but this time he managed to keep the bottle intact. He gave the bottle to his wife, and she was cured in a few days.

Biddy could tell when a neighbour was not a good neighbour or when one man wished ill luck upon another. There was a fairly well-off farmer living near Lissycasey. He had a fine, big herd of cows that gave plenty of milk, so he used to make lots of butter every week.

When May Eve arrived a change came over the butter-making. It started that night when he was churning. No matter how long the man worked at it he could make no butter at all. It continued that way every week from that May Eve until July. The butter just would not come. As time went by, he began to suspect that someone was putting the evil eye on him, so he decided to go and see what Biddy had to say about the matter.

As he reached her house, Biddy met him at the door. Before he could say a single word, Biddy said, 'I know why you have come, and you are right, there is someone taking the butter from you. The worst of it is, that person is someone you think of as a friend, but behind your back he means you no good at all.'

Biddy told him that this 'friend' had a sick calf that would die in two days' time. She told him to watch out between midnight and one o'clock in the morning for where his neighbour would bury the calf.

The man went back home and waited the two days, then stayed up out in the dark night watching his neighbour as Biddy had told him. He saw the neighbour carry the dead calf through into his land, and bury it there.

He said nothing to anyone, but hurried back to Biddy next morning, to see what she would suggest he do next.

'I am afraid that is not the first creature he has buried on your land,' said Biddy.

She told him that his neighbour had been burying animals on his land for some time, and that if he were to look he would find a good number of them there. 'Go home now and tell your neighbour to dig up all the creatures he has buried on your land.'

Biddy went away a moment and returned with a bottle for him. 'Take this bottle and empty it over the place where the animals were buried.'

The man went home and confronted his neighbour. Well, the air was thick with curses and argument, and sticks were shaken and violence threatened, but at last his neighbour did as Biddy had said.

When all the dead animals were removed, and the contents of Biddy's bottle was sprinkled over the soil, it seemed the farmer's luck returned. There was no more trouble with the churning. And the neighbour? He never had much luck afterwards.

❧

If a house or shed was accidentally built over a path that the 'good people' (the fairies) travel, it was understood that bad luck would befall those who live there. This could come as sickness in man or beast living there, loss of wealth or crops.

Biddy told a man whose cattle had stopped giving milk to move a goose cabin that he had put up at the bottom of his field. As soon as he had moved the cabin, the cow's milk flowed freely again.

A poor woman slipped one morning as she as going out the back door of her house and broke her leg. When her husband went to Biddy, she told him they should close that door and use another way in and out, because that was the route the fairies used to go in and out.

There was a man in the west of Clare who built a house on the top of a hill. There was a great view from there; he could see all over the fields, and out to the sea. It was a grand house, but after a very short time living in the new house all his children fell ill, the man's cattle died and he became very poor. He went to see Biddy and asked if she knew why he was beset by such misfortune. Biddy asked the man, 'How could you expect anything else to happen to you when you and your family live on top of another family?'

He asked Biddy, 'What do you mean?'

'You built your house on a path the fairies use, but if you close up one of the rooms in the house, all should go well for you.'

The man did as Biddy said and all his family recovered. They never used that room again, and had no more trouble from the fairies.

I lived in a house like that myself at one time in East Clare, and I was never well there, though it seemed not to affect the men in the family. On my very first night in that house I saw several small men in tall red hats who seemed to be carrying a large human figure wrapped in a sheet upon their shoulders. I watched them pass through the closed front door, cross the kitchen and pass out through the back wall. I later learned there was known to be a fairy path in that area. Ah now, if only Biddy had still been around in

the 1980s, I could have called to her for help. I'm sure she would have known just what to do about it!

Despite her knowledge and her gifts, Biddy could not always save the sick. There was a man called James McInerney who lived in Kilmaley. Around harvest time, he was returning home one evening, after seeing to his stock in the field, when he met an old woman with a shawl pulled up over her head and with no shoes on her feet. He greeted her, thinking she was some poor old wandering woman, but she gave no answer.

When he went home he realised that he had forgotten to close up a certain gap in the field wall through which his stock might be able to escape. So he went back out to close the gap and on his way he met the same woman again. He carried on and when he reached the gap, he found that he had been closed already, but it looked odd to him. The gap appeared to be filled with stones instead of the usual planks of wood lying straight across.

As he was coming back home he once again saw the strange woman. This time she came straight towards him and she reached out to grasp at him. Suddenly he felt very faint. He staggered on and eventually reached his home, but his family were shocked to see his grey face and the life gone out of him. They asked him what had happened and he told them he was afraid for his life because he had met an old fairy woman, and that when he went to the gap it was already blocked.

He took to his bed that night and was there for seven years. His family did not know how to help him, but at last they made up their minds to go to Biddy in Feakle.

It was a long journey, but when they arrived at Biddy's house she greeted them at the door and she told them their names and the place they lived, and who they had met on the way. Biddy listened carefully as they told her their story. Then she looked through her old bottle and thought for a while, and then told them to bring her their hen that slept next to the cock each night. She said that they would probably never be able to bring the hen into her house but they should try it anyhow.

When they got home again James McInerney was still in his bed with no change in him at all. They told him what Biddy had said, and he was pleased to hear that there might yet be a cure for his condition.

The family watched for a few nights to see which hen slept next to the cock each night. Then they caught her and tied her legs with a cord and put her into a basket.

Next day they brought the hen to Biddy's, but just as they reached the door the hen jumped out of the basket and flew away like the wind! They had brought her all that way, so why did she have to run off now? When they went in to Biddy's house she was not at all surprised that the hen was gone. 'Did I not say you would not be able to bring in the hen?' she asked, and told them that the man could not be cured. When she looked into her bottle, she saw the man still in bed as sick as ever. She told them that he would now grow weaker day by day and would die soon after.

When the family got home, the hen was there before them. The man lay tossing and turning feverishly in his bed and he died soon after.

There was a man near Kildysart who had a racehorse that he named 'Biddy Early'. He must have thought calling the horse after Biddy would bring him luck, but the horse had raced often, yet never won a single race. One day, as he was on his way to the races, he met the real Biddy Early herself and asked her why his horse had never won a race. Biddy said that his horse would never win so long as it bore her name. The man changed the horse's name right then and there to 'Jack's Only Daughter' and it won the race that day and the next.

Although her cures and insights were valued by the people, Biddy was not so popular with the priests, who believed she had gained her power from the Devil. A priest in Feakle spoke out against her at one time. He happened to be riding passing her house not long after and Biddy spoke out a few words. His horse bolted into the river and stopped there in the middle, as if its feet were fastened there. The horse would neither go back nor forward, until Biddy spoke again to release it. The priest made his apology, and never spoke another bad word against her.

Despite the misgivings of some of the priests, when Biddy died there was a priest present at her deathbed. To this same priest she gave her blue bottle. They say that he flung it out into the lake below her cottage. There was never a healer like Biddy before or since.

MAIRE RUAD

The tall grey ruin of Leamanagh Castle stands proudly on the road between Inchiquin and Kilfenora. Even today it is impressive, standing like a gateway into the Burren lands.

At one time it was a great mansion with gardens, fishponds and stables, and it straddled strategic travel routes to the west and north of Clare. Leamanagh Castle was the home of a powerful woman, one Mary MacMahon and her husband Conor O'Brien. Mary had sentinels, well-armed, at each of the many gates. These gates would be opened only when it pleased her, and so she controlled the movement of people and trade in that area. The castle could be seen from a mile in all directions, so the people could be in no doubt about who was in charge of the area.

This Mary MacMahon was known locally as Maire Ruad, Maureen Rua, and even Red Moll by the English, for her red hair and her wild, passionate and sometimes cruel nature. Some say that she had seven husbands. Others say it was twenty-five husbands she had, each of them for a just year and a day.

Maire Ruad was a great horsewoman, and it is said that she, along with her husband, rode at the head of her army into battle, like an ancient Celtic queen, and that she was always sure to win. They say that she drove any prisoners she took back home to Leamanagh Castle, and there she executed them herself, by cutting off their heads with an axe. Others say that she was the witch of North Clare, a cruel woman who tortured her servants, hung her maids by the hair from the tower, and killed anyone who got in her way. Mothers used the image of Maire Ruad as a kind

of bogeyman, to frighten children into doing as they were told: 'Maire Ruad will get you, if you don't behave!'

How we see this woman is, of course, determined by our own worldview. She was for sure a powerful woman, unashamed of her sexuality, lover of the wild Burren landscape, the cliffs and her black stallion; she would do whatever was necessary to preserve her lands for her children – even if that meant marrying the enemy. And it seems that Maire Ruad did all these things.

A mother had a son who had acquired no manners and would do nothing he was told. This woman brought her son to Leamanagh Castle, so that he would learn some manners and become civilised. When she brought the boy to the door of the castle, Maire Ruad took him inside and told his mother to come back for him in a week's time, when she'd hear no more cheek from him. The mother went home and life was quiet there without him. When the week was over, she returned to the castle. The servant showed her into the grand room where Maire Ruad received her. 'So, how are his manners now?' asked the woman.

'I have not heard a word of disobedience from him,' said Maire Ruad, and told her she would find her son up in the tower. The woman climbed the steps in the tower, and when she reached the top, she found her son – hanging from a rafter, and quite dead.

Maire Ruad's husband, Conor O'Brien, was mortally wounded in a battle against General Ireton. Maire Ruad's army brought him back on a stretcher to Leamanagh Castle. Maire Ruad watched from the battlements as they approached and neither spoke nor wept. When they asked her what to do with her husband, she called down from the tower, 'What do I want with dead men here?'

When they told her that Conor was in fact still alive, she tended him herself and nursed him gently until he breathed his last. Her grief and tears were fierce, as Conor O'Brien had been the one true love of her life.

She dressed herself in her finest gown and jewels and ordered a coach and horses to take her to the gates of Limerick. It was night when she neared the city, which was held by General Ireton. A guard stopped her coach and asked angrily what business she had there. Maire Ruad wept, shouted and cursed at the guard, making so much noise that Ireton and his officers, who were dining at the time, came out to see what was causing the disturbance. 'Who is this woman, screaming like a banshee at our gates?' they asked.

'I was Conor O'Brien's wife yesterday, and today I am his widow,' said Maire Ruad.

'Conor O'Brien fought us bravely just yesterday. Now you say that he is dead. Can you prove this? Where is his body?'

'I buried my husband this morning. Here is your proof: I am a widow now, and I will marry any one of your officers who will ask me,' she said.

One Captain Cooper, who was a brave man, stepped forward, bent his knee and proposed marriage. They were married then, and so it was that Maire Ruad preserved the O'Brien lands for her sons, whom she had advised to surrender to Ireton's army. Maire Ruad had her revenge. She sought out, captured and hanged the man who had shot her first husband.

Her marriage to Cooper was not a happy one, and they argued one morning, he saying some insult against Connor O'Brien. Had he known her better, he might not have spoken so slightingly of the husband she had truly loved. Maire Ruad leapt from her bed and gave Cooper so forceful a kick in his stomach that he died from the blow.

❧

Maire Ruad had a black stallion, a magnificent horse, coveted by many. It was a half-wild creature, like herself. Rumours said that the horse was blind, and that she had trained the animal to carry a rider to the edge of the Cliffs of Moher, and there to halt suddenly. The rider would be thrown over the edge and fall to their certain death in the rough Atlantic waters below.

One day, a man with a splendid physique caught Maire Ruad's eye. She commanded this handsome fellow to come to her the following morning for an audience. The man went home and told his sad story. Having heard the stories of Maire Ruad's short-lived fancy-men, he feared that she had trouble in store for him. Would she make him ride her wild black stallion? That would surely mean he would end his day on the jagged rocks or in the foaming waters below the Cliffs of Moher.

A man sitting by the fire said, 'Ah, Sean, I have an idea. We will change clothes, and I will go in your place.' This man was a great jockey, and was sure he would manage the black horse. So in the morning the two men changed clothes and the new 'Sean' went to the castle.

Maire Ruad greeted him there and ordered him to get up on the horse. She told 'Sean' that if he came home alive, he could have the horse, and that she would make him her husband. The creature was wild, indeed, but 'Sean' leapt up on its back and dug his spurs into its sides.

As soon as the horse felt the spurs, it bolted, heading over the grass and grey rock towards the sea. 'Sean' held on for dear life. Every time the horse slackened pace, 'Sean' dug his spurs in deeper, thinking he could tire out the animal and eventually master it. Instead, to his dismay, it seemed that the horse found new strength each time, and rode on with a fresh burst of energy, still heading the direction of the cliffs. At last they reached the cliffs and 'Sean' let the horse have its own way until it was about to reach the cliff edge. Just as the horse approached the precipice, the man pulled so hard on the reins that the bit tore the jawbone of the horse and it fell dead. They say that the imprint of the stallion's footprints can still be seen on the rocks at the edge of the Cliffs of Moher.

Still a passionate woman, Maire Ruad took another husband following Cooper's death. And yet another. They say she took a series of men, some for just a year and a day, after which she had them killed, claiming that she had found them cavorting with her serving maid.

Maire Ruad violent lifestyle finally caught up with her and people say that she was taken by her enemies and ended her days fastened up in a hollow tree. Her red-haired ghost is said to haunt the road before the castle.

THE HAG OF BEALAHA

Down in the west of Clare there was once a ferocious woman known as Cailleach Bealaha, or The Hag of Bealaha. She was a known danger to travellers on this particular stretch of road. The hag was said to live in Bealaha Fort, an overgrown lios or ringfort by the side of the road. In a roadside fence there is a white stone with a hollow that is said to be her chair, where she would sit and wait for a victim to pass. Nearby are some large stones she is said to have dropped from her apron as she flew across the sky.

Behind every ancient and hideous hag, there is usually a young and beautiful girl who has been insulted, mistreated or abused. 'Hell hath no fury like a woman scorned,' so says the old saying. The Cailleach Bealaha is no exception. Although her name may be lost, she was not always an ugly old woman with a taste for vengeance. She was once a young woman, who lived with her two sisters in a house by the strand near Bealaha. She was about to be married, and there was to be a great party at the house. She sent a servant to fetch water from a well nearby that was known to be enchanted. A heavy flagstone lid was always kept on this well, for it was known that if was left uncovered it would overflow. The servant fetched the bucket of water, but in all the hurry and bustle of the wedding party, she forgot to put the flagstone cover back on the well. The water began to overflow. The water rose higher and higher, foaming and spilling out over the edge of the well. It rose higher still higher, covering the field and rising to the door of the grand house itself. When the water reached the ballroom, panic ensued. The young bridegroom and his family and friends leapt onto their horses and rode off to save themselves. In his haste the bridegroom thought nothing of his intended bride, whom he left behind to save herself, if she could. She struggled as her long white wedding gown grew heavy with the flood and the waters dragged her down and down. She called out for her bridegroom to help her, but he was far away by then. She realised that he had left her to drown, and she swore that she would forever after haunt men and lure them to their death. The place where the house had been is now under the waters of Farrihy Lake.

Every night after dark she would come out onto the road and wait for any man on a horse to come by that way. The people of the area would warn travellers and strangers about the danger, but if a man was unfortunate enough to be travelling that way after dark, the Cailleach Bealaha would leap up behind him on the horse and crush or choke him to death. Many a man lost his life at the hand of the Cailleach Bealaha.

She spent her days spinning in the old lios by the roadside. People mostly left her alone, as they knew her reputation, but one day, a young man threw stones at her as she sat spinning. She leapt to her feet, shaking her fist at him, shouting curses and swearing, 'Ha ha, I will get you yet!' A time came when that young man's father was dying and he was sent out after dark to fetch the priest from Kilrush. A shopkeeper warned him to beware of the hag, and gave him a black-handled knife. 'Do not be afraid to use the knife if the hag jumps up behind you on your horse. If you do not, she will kill you for sure.'

He was nervously riding along the road that passes the lios, and the hag leapt up behind him on his horse. She clung to him fiercely, stretching her bony arms around his chest and his throat. He coughed and struggled. She was surely going to choke him to death! He reached into his pocket for the black-handled knife and struck her with it.

The hag fell from the horse and called, 'Pull out the knife and stick it in again.'

But the young man said, 'No!' and left the knife stuck into the hag, and rode on his way, leaving her for dead.

The next morning, there was the black-handled knife lying by the roadside. But there was no sign of the hag. All that remained of the Cailleach Bealaha was a heap of grey slime and ashes. She never bothered any man on that road again. They buried what was left of her at the side of the road, and each person who passed placed another stone on her grave, lest she should rise again.

GRIAN, DAUGHTER OF THE SUN

Long before the time of Christ, there lived a girl of royal blood whose name was Grian. Her father was a powerful chieftain from the Slieve Aughty Mountains in East Clare. Grian had never known her mother. They called her Grian of the Bright Cheeks, for her face shone with the radiance and brightness of the sun. As she grew to become a young woman, many lads fell in love with her, which was hardly surprising, given her unearthly beauty. There was one, however, who was more serious than the others and wanted to marry her. Perhaps that was when the trouble started, because he needed to know Grian's pedigree.

Grian had never had any curiosity about her identity before, but now she begged her father to tell her about her mother. Under pressure from his daughter, he revealed that her mother was in fact a sunbeam, and not a human woman at all!

To say that Grian was shocked is an understatement! She was beside herself with grief and sunk into a deep depression. Would any young man want to marry her, once he learned of her extraordinary origins? She thought not. The distraught young woman threw herself into the waters of the lake that now bears her name, Lough Graney. Grian was drowned in the lough and her body was carried by the river that flows from it. She was washed ashore at a place now called Derrygraney near to an oak wood between Scariff and Lough Derg.

When they discovered her body there and saw the beauty of her face, even in death, her friends brought her to Tuamgraney, where they buried her under a mound that can still be seen in the grounds of the old Glebe House. Her name was put on the village that grew up around it, Tuamgraney – the tomb of Grian, the sun maiden.

A few miles from Lough Graney there is a holy well called Tober Grainne, or Grian's Well.

MAL AND CUCHULAINN

Way back in the mists of time, the bold young Cuchulainn, son of the sun god Lugh, champion and protector of Ulster, was on his travels around the country, doing brave deeds. Amongst his many notable attributes, Cuchulainn was known for his ability to leap like a salmon. He would twist and turn and still manage to land safely on rocky precipices and narrow bridges. His name was given to crags and rocks from the Cuillin Mountains on the Isle of Skye, where he trained with the warrior-woman Scatach, to Loop Head in the south-western edge of County Clare.

Wherever the champion went, there was always the danger that women would fall in love with him. They could hardly help themselves, given that he was such a fine figure of a lad. He may have been short of stature, but he was fit, young and handsome, his brown hair streaked with red and golden highlights.

There was a woman named Mal who knew the arts of magic, and she had set her sights on the young Cuchulainn. She followed him wherever he went, pursuing him with her charm and her arts. She dressed herself in her finest silks, draped herself with jewels, made herself beautiful and interesting, but despite all her beguiling looks and her willingness, and despite her magic spells, Cuchulainn was simply just not interested. How could he get this message through to Mal?

Though he snubbed her when she tried to speak to him; though he turned away, Mal refused to give up her pursuit of the young warrior. She followed him wherever he went. Wherever he set his foot, she would walk behind him, so close she was like his shadow.

Cuchulainn took to getting up early and running as fast as he could, and he was fleet of foot. Mal, being no athlete herself, used her magic to keep up with him.

Mal followed him the length of County Clare, all the way down to the Loop Head Peninsula. Cuchulainn was still running until he reached the point where there was no place left to run. The long finger of land had come to its end. Looking over his shoulder, Cuchilainn saw sea birds wheel and turn in the sky above, and behind him saw Mal still in pursuit. He threw himself into the air and leapt from the land's end to a tall pillar of rock that stood alone in the wild foaming waves. 'Do not follow me, witch! The distance is too great for you to leap,' Cuchulainn warned her.

Summoning her magic arts, Mal followed him onto the small craggy island, crying, 'Now I have you, my darling boy. Surrender, Cuchulainn, and let me be your love!'

'Never!' yelled Cuchulainn, as he turned on his heel, and leapt again, back to the finger of rock that was the mainland.

Mal followed him but, in the heat of the moment, she took no time to prepare herself for this more difficult jump. Her leap fell short of the mainland, and Mal fell screaming in disbelief, as her unrequited love turned to rage and to despair. Her body was dashed against the cliffs as it fell and landed crumpled and broken on the rocks below. When the waves carried her body out to sea, her blood turned the blue-green waters red all the way from Loop Head to Hag's Head, which was her home.

Mal's story may be largely forgotten, but her name lives on in Milltown Malbay, where her broken body was washed ashore. At Hag's Head, further up the coast, you can see in the rocks the face of an old hag facing out to sea.

Cuchullain was not forgotten, for Loop Head, as we know it now, was once named Leap Head after his famous jump.

MURDER, MONARCHY AND MONG THE FAIR

Mong Finn the Fair Haired was the daughter of the King of Munster sometime in the fourth century AD. Her brother, Crimthan Mac Fidach, would become Ard Ri, that is the High King of Ireland. Family relationships, it seems, have not always been simple. Sharing parentage has been no guarantee of friendly kinship, not least when there is power and succession to a crown at stake.

Mong Finn the Fair Haired married Eochaidh Muigh-Medon, High King of Ireland, but Eochaidh also had another wife, Carthann, who was dark haired. That both wives lived within the court at the same time surely led to some unrest in the home. Both wives fulfilled their obligations to the king. Mong Fion bore Eochaidh four sons: Brian, Fiachra, Ailill and Fergus; while Carthann bore only the one son, Niall, who was Eochaidh's favourite. Niall was the one he would like to follow him into the kingship, much to the chagrin of Mong Finn, who had hoped that her eldest son Brian would succeed his father as Ard Ri.

Mong Finn, a king's daughter, was a strong and wilful woman, determined to see her bloodline maintain the sovereignty. She worked quietly behind the scenes, spreading gossip about Carthann. She spoke persuasively, suggesting to Eochaidh that he should send his favourite son, Niall, to be fostered away from the court. She insisted it would be the making of the boy, and put pressure on Eochaidh until he agreed. Once the boy was gone from her sight, Mong Finn asserted her position as senior wife and made Carthann her servant. Mong Finn gave Carthann the most menial of tasks, such as carrying water to the court, not simply demoting her, but adding the salt of mockery to the wound.

Niall was fostered by a poet sympathetic to his father's cause. The poet saw to it that Niall was cared for and he educated the boy himself, so that he would be fit to return to court when the right time came. When the young prince came of age, the poet presented him to the court, where Eochaidh received him back into his household with delight. Niall lost no time in restoring his mother's position at court. Mong Finn no doubt simmered with anger, while dreaming up ways to overcome these new obstacles to her son's accession.

Mong Finn did not act hastily, but waited until Eochaidh's death. Then she used her power and political influence to ensure the outcome she desired: her brother Crimthan would wear the crown until her son Brian was of an age to take the throne. Mong Finn could now relax her guard, for it seemed that she had managed to secure her son's succession. Or so she thought. Do you know the saying: if you want to give God a laugh, tell him your plans? Well, Mong Finn's plans did not turn out quite as she had expected.

Crimthan proved himself a good and strong ruler, and a popular one at that. He led campaigns in Ireland and abroad, against the Picts, Britons and Romans, in Scotland, Britain and in Gaul, and won fame and bounty for his people. He became a successful and a popular ruler with a strong following in the country. Perhaps this unexpected turn of events is what drove Mong Finn to do what she did next.

Mong Finn plotted to kill her own brother, but she did this in a way that would leave her family untarnished by the finger of suspicion. While the court was travelling through

Clare, she prepared a poison and secretly mixed it into a drink. When they stopped to eat on the hillside above Cratloe, she presented one goblet to Crimthan and took a second one herself. Pouring the drink, Mong Finn praised and toasted her brother, then raised her goblet to her lips and drank. Assuming that there must therefore be no harm in the drink, the king also drank. Shortly afterwards he collapsed on that hillside in the agonies of death. That very spot is called to this day Slieve Oighe an Ri, the Mountain of the King's Death. A cairn was raised there, known today as the King's Grave.

Mong Finn died too from her self-administered poison, and was buried at King's Island in Limerick. All her scheming and politicking had been in vain, for the popular choice was that Niall succeed to the throne. This same Niall went on to become the famous Niall of the Nine Hostages.

A WITTY WIFE

The Goban Saor was a carpenter mason and smith who lived in Ireland long ago. He was a real person, who lived about a hundred years after St Patrick. He was a skilled craftsman with a fine eye for every detail and he could turn his hand to work with wood or stone or metal. His services were sought after by saints and princes throughout the land of Ireland and far beyond these shores. They say that there was not a church nor castle of any importance built in Ireland that he did not have a hand in the building of. Although stories about the Goban Saor and his adventures are widespread throughout the country, these versions claim that he lived in Querrin.

The Goban Saor was married and his wife was going to have a baby. He already had several daughters, but he was still holding out hope for a son. He was leaving to go and do some building job, and he turned to his wife and said, 'If it is another daughter you have this time, I'll kill you when I come back!' He was a man of considerable wit and only meant it as a joke, but his wife was worried, knowing that when the time came, it would be another girl that was born. There was a neighbour woman having a child at the same time, and hers was a boy, so the two women exchanged their babies in the hope this would keep the Goban Saor happy.

As the boy child grew, he seemed slow to learn, and the Goban suspected this might be no son of his. He tried to teach him all he knew, but the boy lacked interest or skill, and preferred to dream his days away. The men said that the boy knew nothing about building at all. One man had asked him to make a wedge for him. The boy asked where it was to go. When the man put his finger on the spot, the boy hit the wedge with his mallet and caught the man's finger so tight with it, there was no way to get it out again.

When the boy was grown, the Goban thought to compensate for his son's lack of wit by marrying him to a woman with plenty of it.

At this time the Goban Saor had a house in Querrin, and another along the shore in Doonaha. He would spend part of the year in one and part of the year in the other, when he was not travelling about the country seeing to the building of great churches and so on.

The Goban told his son to go to the fair and to find himself a witty wife. 'How will I know her?'

'Take this sheepskin with you to the fair,' said the Goban, 'and sell it, but bring me back the skin, and the price of the skin.'

The lad was puzzled. What in all the heavens did his father mean? How could he bring back the skin and the price of it? It didn't make any sense, even to him, who was used to things making no sense. The lad walked from stall to stall, asking the skin and the price of it, and everybody laughed at the poor foolish boy with no wit nor sense. At last he sat down, with the skin in his hands and his mouth curling down in weary resignation. A lively girl came up and asked him what was bothering him.

'My father told me to sell this skin, and bring him back the skin and the price of it,' said the lad. 'I have asked everyone, but they only laugh at me.'

The girl's bright face creased open in a laugh. 'Ha! We will see who is laughing soon. Give it here,' she said. She took up a pair of shears and cut the wool off of the sheepskin and put it in her bag. 'Here is the skin,' she said handing him back the shaved hide, 'and here is the price of it. Take that to your father with my regards.'

When he got home and gave his father the skin and the money, the Goban was certainly impressed. 'Do you know where this girl lives?' he asked.

'Her family is down by the shore.'

'Take her this message from me. Tell her to come here to meet me tomorrow. Tell her she must come not in daylight, and yet not by night; to come not by the road and not over the fields; and not alone but with no other person.'

The Goban Saor's son duly delivered the message. He knew by now that this was one very smart girl, and if anyone could figure out his father's instructions, she was the one to do it.

The next day, just as the sinking sun was painting the sky with twilight colours, the girl arrived at the Goban Saor's door. She came walking along the top of the hedge, and she had with her a small shaggy terrier dog. The Goban was satisfied that she was clearly a woman of wit and wisdom, and he gave her his blessing to marry his son.

Once he was a married man, the son went out working each day with his father. One day when they had many miles to walk to the work, the Goban told his son to shorten the road.

'I cannot do that,' said the son.

'Well, you might as well go home now,' says the Goban, so the son turned and walked back the way they had come.

When his clever wife asked why he had returned, he told her he did not know how to shorten the road for his father. She clapped her hands together and smiled, 'You must run back along the road, and when you catch up with your father, tell him a story.'

Her husband did as she suggested. When he met up with his father, he began to tell a story, and of course one story opened a doorway into another. The tales were all so interesting and varied and full of adventure and pathos and humour, that both men laughed or wept or sighed, and neither was aware of the many miles they travelled that day. Just as they reached the end of their journey, the long story began to find its ending, just as this one has.

A PALACE IN SCOTLAND

Word of the Goban Saor's exceptional talents spread far and wide. Soon he was receiving invitations to come and design and build palaces and cathedrals for kings in Scotland, Wales, England and even as far as the lands of the Northmen.

The King of Scotland sent for him to come and build a palace. The Goban and his son travelled together, and no doubt many stories were told on that long journey.

Before they left, the son's clever wife advised him to befriend the Scottish king's daughter, 'It always pays to have a friend at court,' she told him as they parted. He made sure to do this, and the girl proved only too willing to spend time in the Goban's son's company. The two took long walks together by the river and shared confidences. The Goban's son was only too happy to foster this new friendship, in fact, perhaps more than was fitting for a recently married man, but that would be another story altogether.

After a year had passed, the building of the palace was nearly complete. It was spectacularly beautiful, with its arches and cornices, its flowing curves and carvings. There was only one small job to finish up near the roof. The King's daughter confided in the Goban's son that her father wished his palace to be the only one of its kind. She said, 'He will not permit your father and yourself to return to Ireland, lest he should build another palace as beautiful as his.'

The Goban, being a man of considerable wit, found a way to take his leave. He told the King that there was a very particular tool he needed to complete the work, and that he must go home to Querrin to collect this instrument.

The King, being no fool, refused to let him go. 'Not at all, my good craftsman, your skills are needed here. I simply cannot spare you at this crucial time in the proceedings. Rather we shall send our own son to collect the instrument you require.'

'Your son will not know where to find it, sir,' said the Goban. 'Let me give him a description of the tool I need. Its name is ...'

He wrote the words: 'When it is open, close it', on a slip of paper, and turned to the King's son. 'My son's wife will help you to find it if you give her this note when you arrive in Querrin.'

'How will I know the house?' asked the King's son.

'It has a door at the front and another at the side.' said the Goban, describing almost any house he might see.

The King's son set off, wondering about this strange tool. Perhaps it was some particular kind of vice?

Sometime later he arrived in the west of Ireland and found his way to the Goban's house. He asked the son's clever wife for the instrument the Goban needed, and handed her the note. She smiled in welcome and offered him some refreshment, then brought him into the Goban's tool store. She indicated a particular press saying, 'You will find what you are looking for in here. I believe it is at the bottom of this press.'

She unlocked it and raised the heavy lid. As the King's son leant over to search for the instrument at the bottom of the deep chest, the clever young woman tilted him over into the press and locked it behind him. The Prince knocked and shouted, but all in vain. She wrote a letter to the Scottish King telling him what she had done and that his son was now her hostage until her own two men should return home.

When he read the letter, the Scottish King admitted she had bested him. 'That is one clever girl you have there in Ireland. Go on away home to her now, and send my boy back home to me with a clip round his ear for his stupidity!'

The Goban and his son set themselves back on the road home, and another good number of stories they no doubt shared on their way.

References:

Biddy Early: I heard stories about Biddy Early all over East Clare, from sources long since forgotten. Also, from the Schools Folklore Scheme (1937-38) (hereafter referred to as SFS), Alfred Coffey, Meelick School, p.269; Mrs Murphy,

Maghera, Tulla; Maureen Brassil, Poulaphuca, Ballynacally, told by Mrs and Mr James Brassil; Mary O'Brien, told by Mrs O'Brien, Quin; James Meaney, Quin; Peggy O'Conor told by Mrs Katherine O'Connor, Musichill, Lissycasey, p.208; John Malloy, Cappaleigh told to Christina Malloy, Inch, p.3; Eily Shannon, Ballynacally, told by Margaret Shannon.

Maire Ruad: SFS (1937-38) Micheal O Catain, Ennis, p.174, Scoil na mBrathar, Ennis; SFS (1937-38) Sean O Halloran, Scoil na mBrathar, p.251; Thomas J. Westropp, *Folklore of Clare* (Ennis; CLASP Press, 2000).

The Hag of Bealaha: SFS (1937-38) Michael Foley, told to Mary Hennessey, Tullycrine.

Murder, Monarchy and Mong the Fair: D. O'Riain and S. O'Cinneide, *The History and Folklore of Parteen and Meelick* (Limerick, 1990).

A Witty Wife: SFS (1937-38) Mrs Flanagan, told to P. Melican, Tullycrine NS.

A Palace in Scotland: SFS (1937-38) Frances Keane heard it from John Kitson, Querrin.

2

THE BLACKSMITH

THE BLACKSMITH'S CURE

The blacksmith has always been a powerful figure in myth and legend. It is hardly surprising that someone who had command of the mysteries of fire to transform iron would have a special role in traditional cultures, and could be thought to have other powers that might be considered miraculous too.

There is a family by name of Curtis, or Curtin, in the Kilnaboy area that have a reputation for having a cure for liver disease, bleeding, and cows who swallow potatoes. This cure is passed on from one generation to the next, since the day, long ago, when the Kilnaboy blacksmith did a great service that saved the life of someone in dire need. Some say it was Saint Patrick himself that the blacksmith helped; others say that it was a priest during the penal times whose life he saved; but all are clear that the cure was given to Curtis as a blessing, in thanks for a service rendered in time of need. Here is one version of the story:

A long time ago there was a blacksmith living in Kilnaboy by the name of Curtin. His forge was in a hut that stood by the side of the road, convenient for anyone passing by. The smith worked there every day despite the fact that he was not in the best of health. For a blacksmith, he was not the strongest of men, as he suffered from the liver complaint.

One fine morning, as he worked in the forge, Curtin saw a horseman coming towards him at a gallop. The horse was lathered in sweat and dust, the rider gaunt, ragged, filthy and drawn. Both looked exhausted, as if the hounds of Hell were at their heels and would soon catch up with them.

Horse and rider came to stop in front of the forge and the man dismounted.

'A blessing on you good smith, if you would shoe my horse, and quickly, in the name of God.'

The smith investigated the horse's damaged shoe, and watched the worried face of the rider, who was constantly looking over his shoulder. He agreed to shoe the horse and set about his work.

While he was shaping the metal he noticed that the man's hands were shaking, and his breathing was fast and irregular.

Curtin asked, 'What is wrong with you, man? Are you unwell, sir? I can't help but notice you seem to be terribly afraid of something.'

The man replied 'I am a priest and I am being hunted like a dog by the English. I have been fleeing from them for three days now, and still they are close behind me. I cannot keep on riding like this, nor can my horse keep up this pace. I greatly fear that it will not be long before they catch me, and God help me if they do!'

The smith felt sorry for the hunted priest. By his eyes and his demeanour, he could see the priest was a good man,

and he wished he could think of a way to help him. After a while he came up with a cunning plan.

He turned to the priest and said, 'Bring in your horse.'

The smith removed all four of the horse's shoes, turned them back to front and nailed them on again.

The priest looked baffled, until the smith explained his plan, ' Now, when your horse travels in this direction, anyone who sees the tracks will think it is going the opposite way.'

The priest was delighted and shook his hand and thanked him very much, saying he wished that he could do something for him in exchange for his kindness.

As he made ready to leave, the priest asked Curtin if he was suffering from any disease.

'I have the 'Liver Complaint',' said the smith.

'When you wake next morning, you will find yourself cured,' said the priest. 'And more than that, this blessing will pass from you to your descendants, so that always your family will always have the cure. People will come to you to cure their liver disease, and you will always have a way to earn a living.'

Since that day, many people have been cured by this gift of the Curtins of Kilnaboy.

The sick person lies on an anvil and the smith pretends to strike him three times with his hammer, after which the patient must drink forge water. A person going for the cure needs to go on two Mondays and a Thursday. The man who has the cure now (in the late 1930s) is called Robert Curtin.

AN GABA RUAD

The blacksmith has always been a figure of fascination and has often been accredited with unusual powers, sometimes as a healer, other times as a go-between with the fairies and other unseen forces.

There was a man named Melican who lived in the townland of Cahercanivan near Kilmihil. He was known in the area as 'The Gaba Ruad', or 'Goweru', because he was a blacksmith by trade and had red hair. His forge was by a crossroads that is still known as the Gaba Ruad's Cross, although a different house is there now.

People said that the Goweru had a habit of 'going with the fairies', and that he was a master of all the 'holy travellers' or ghosts. The reputation of his uncanny gift of prophecy and other remarkable powers meant many of his neighbours were afraid of him.

The Goweru would often disappear for several days at a time. No one could say where he had gone, nor why. Those with less of an imagination would say that he had taken to his bed. Wherever it was he went, when he returned he could tell his customers and neighbours all manner of secret things that had happened to them or their families.

He told one man about a letter he had received in the last few days, from a relative in America informing him of his brother's death there. He told him that he had become heir to a small fortune – a fact that the man had chosen to keep secret from his neighbours for the meantime. He told other people about perils that would befall them on a certain date. Sometimes it was good news that he told about. Whatever he said, his prophecies always came true, and so people were careful not to offend him in case he would set his friends, the fairies, or 'good people', against them. Because of his clients' fears, the forge was always busy, and no one would dare to quarrel over whatever he charged for his services.

When he was absent from the forge, people said he was travelling with the good people, or living with them within the green hills. As soon as he returned, he could tell his neighbours if one of them had gone to another blacksmith, even for a small job, like putting in a single nail to a horse's hoof. He would punish them, saying they would not do it again. He would put a spell on them then, so that their horses would then run lame. The other blacksmiths would refuse to help them for fear of the Goweru's anger.

He was a great judge of horses, and could tell his neighbours to the penny what price would be offered for their horses at the next fair, and whether they would accept the price.

He would also tell them tales from his travels with the fairies, tell what he had seen the night before. He would describe how he had seen a particular white cow in a certain spot in their field that night.

One night, a party of horsemen came to wake him when he was asleep in his bed. They told him to get up and make ready to ride with them. He had no horse himself, so they told him to climb onto a plough that lay outside the wall of the forge. He mounted the plough and it rose up, carrying him along with the party of horsemen as they flew over ditches and dykes, riding through the night. In the morning he was deposited back at the forge and took to his bed for the day.

Later that day a beggar man came to his door, asking for a place to rest for the night. The Goweru welcomed him in and gave the poor man a place to sleep. He noticed the beggar getting weaker and more weary as each hour passed. 'Are you sick, man?' he asked, but the beggar said 'No'.

'Should I fetch you the priest?' asked the blacksmith.

'No, no, it's late. It will keep till the morning.'

But the Goweru feared the man would not last so long, and went out in the night to fetch the priest. The priest gave the poor man the last rites, and he died a few hours later.

Some months later, that same old man's ghost appeared at the forge late one night. The man asked, 'You were kind to me, blacksmith. Is there something I can do for you? What do you want? Ask me, and I will give it.'

The Goweru asked, 'Answer me this: What sort of place is the otherworld?'

The old man said, 'It is a good man that will have the sheltery side of the ditch earned for himself on the Last Day'.

THE MYSTERIOUS BLACKSMITH

There was at one time a blacksmith working around Mount Callan, whose life was a complete mystery to the people there. If you asked, no one could tell you where he lived. No one could give you directions to the forge. No one ever saw him at work. Despite all the mystery, the work still got done. The smith shod horses and he made whatever tools the farmers in the area needed.

One day, as the smith was walking along, he saw a number of soldiers on horseback coming along the road. He could see that the horse the general rode was very lame. The general called out to him, asking did he know was there if a forge anywhere nearby that he could get his horse shod.

The smith answered, 'I do not. But if you will break the horse's leg and give to me the shin bone and the hoof, I will bring it back to you shod, and the horse will be none the worse after it.'

The general was mystified, but as the horse was lame anyway, he did as the smith said. The horse lay down on the ground and looked asleep. The smith took the shin and hoof and said he'd be back in twenty minutes time.

When he came back he had a new shoe on the horse's hoof. He put the two parts of the horse's leg together and said some words no one could understand. As soon as he did, the horse woke up, shook itself and stood up on its four legs again, good as new.

The general was delighted with the work done well and quickly. He asked the man what he owed the smith for his work. The smith answered, 'He takes no money.'

'Well, what is this smith's name?'

'Mairtin Liam Gaba,' said the smith, and was gone as quick as a flash.

References:

The Blacksmith's Cure: SFS (1937-38) Patrick McGuane, Scumhall, Corofin, County Clare, p.57, Diseart.

An Gaba Ruad: SFS (1937-38) Thomas Madigan, Burrane Lower, Burrane School, p.12; John O'Dea, told to Thomas MacDonnell, Tullycrine NS p.64.

The Mysterious Blacksmith: SFS (1937-38) Michael Donlan, Caherush.

3

LON MAC LIOFA

LON MAC LIOFA THE SMITH

Long ago, before the time of even the earliest ancestors of
the Irish, in the time of the Tuatha De Danaan, there was
a smith named Lon Mac Liofa, one of the De Danaans
himself, and therefore bound to be gifted in some way, as
all those good folk were. Lon Mac Liofa was the first man
in the whole land of Ireland to make an edged weapon.
Perhaps it was as well that he had such skills, for his looks
were strange. The smith had only one leg, but what he
lacked in the way of feet, he made up for by having three
hands: two in their usual places at the end of each arm,
and a third that grew out from the centre of his chest. This
extra limb proved very handy indeed, and the smith used it
for holding the metal on the anvil as he wielded hammers
and worked it into spearheads and swords with his two
other hands. The single leg proved no handicap either, as
the smith travelled around the country by springing with

a great bounding leap, and could be seen flying from place to place through the air.

Now, we all know that the De Danaans were too fond of the lovely island of Ireland to leave it when the next crowd of incomers from across the waves challenged them. So when the Milesians landed and wanted to settle here, the De Danaans chose to live underground in the green hills, rather than leave the land they loved. They became the fairy folk. Only Lon Mac Liofa stayed, in his cave on the mountain of Sliabh na Glaise, and continued his work as smith to the new people. Before this, the weapons were bronze or stone, but these new people wanted swords of iron, and of course Lon Mac Liofa knew how to work with the new metal.

As time went on, Lon Mac Liofa longed to do some smithwork for a worthy warrior chief. At last he heard about the mighty warrior Fionn MacCumhall, and wondered if perhaps he could use the services of a talented craftsman. Lon Mac Liofa set off to present himself at Fionn's court, which at that time was on the Hill of Howth. He sprang across the hills and valleys from west to east on his single leg, which of course took him no time at all. When he reached the gates of Fionn's camp, the gateman challenged him, as was only to be expected. 'What is your name, and what is your business here?'

'I am Lon Mac Liofa of the Tuatha De Danaan. I am a master smith by trade and profession, and I lay a geasa on your master, that his people could not overtake me in a race to my own forge at Mohernagartan on Slievenaglasha.' Having laid down his challenge, Lon Mac Liofa turned heel and bounded off swiftly in a westward direction. The gateman shook his head in confusion at what he had seen. Had he really seen a strange figure from an earlier time? A one-legged, three-handed figure from the ancient race of magicians and wizards? Scratching his head and rubbing his eyes, he knew he must relate the strange news immediately to Fionn. A geasa, after all, is an obligation and must be fulfilled.

Perhaps he thought no one could overtake him, but one of Fionn's party, a young man named Caoilté of the slender hard legs, reached the entrance to the forge just as Lon Mac Liofa did himself.

'That was a close race, Smith! Let us go in together,' said Caoilte, slapping the smith on the back.

'You are welcome, Caoilté of the Slender Hard Legs, welcome to my forge! You rose to meet my challenge, and you need fear no magic spells from me. I brought you here so that I can make sturdy iron weapons – sharp swords and spears – for Fionn and his warriors, that will win great fame and fortune for you all with their deeds of valour.' The Lon sighed, 'Ah, how I have missed the work all these quiet years!'

Caoilté worked alongside Lon Mac Liofa in his forge for three days, before Fionn and seven other warriors arrived. Fionn admired the workmanship and the balance of the eight swords that were wrought already.

Two of Fionn's warriors, Conan and Goll, were keen to learn the art of blacksmithing, and each of them made a few swords, but they struck the anvil with the sledge so powerfully that they broke it in two!

LON MAC LIOFA'S COW

The King of Spain used to have a cow that gave so much milk that it could fill the biggest vessel in the world. This marvellous beast was offered as a prize in a competition to find the best athlete in the world. It must have been a bit like the Olympics are today, with athletes coming from every corner to try their luck and test their skill. Lon Mac Liofa bounded his way to Spain and he won the cow. He brought the cow, whose name was the Glas Gaibreac, the grey-green cow, back home. Lon had seven sons and he gave them the job of caring for the cow, one of them each day of the week. They let her roam the fields by day, and shut her in a cow-house for the night. They held the cow by the tail as she grazed, until she reached the rim of the plateau. Then they would turn her around and she would graze her way back to the cow house. All around, the rocks are marked with her hoof prints, and they can be seen to this day.

Now the king of that place had three sons who came to Lon Mac Liofa wanting the finest of iron swords. Lon Mac Liofa asked them to see that the Glas was watered while he was busy in his forge. The king's sons had their own cattle to see to, but said they would water his cow when they returned. The smith warned them to mind the cow, not to strike her, and to be sure to bring her back safely. The boys drew lots for it, and it was the youngest who had to do the work. He had to pull the Glas by her tail to the seven streams of Taosca before she could get enough water to drink.

On his way back, as he passed by the forge, he could hear his brothers arguing about which was the finest sword. They picked up each one, weighed it in their hands, swung them around, then chose the best swords for themselves, saying, 'Our youngest brother can have the worst!' and they laughed. Mad with anger, the youngest, forgetting the smith's warning, lashed out and struck the cow, and rushed into the smith's house.

'Where is my cow?' Lon Mac Liofa asked. 'Is she well and watered?'

'She is outside,' said the boy, but when the smith went out the cow could not be seen. The Glas had disappeared back to Spain!

The king's son swore that he would not rest nor sleep until he had got the cow back again, and he set off at once for Spain. The King of Spain set him three tasks to do if he wanted to get back the cow for Lon Mac Liofa.

The first deed was to eat a firkin and 700 firkins of the same cow's butter with the breadth of his ear of bread. For the second deed he had to tan a hide and 700 hides as smooth as the glove in his hand. The third deed was to get the spancil off the cow.

The boy wondered, 'How will I ever manage to eat a firkin and 700 firkins of butter on that small piece of bread? How can I tan a hide and 700 hides?' He thought it was hopeless, but he asked for help from an old witch. The old woman gave him a rusty iron knife and said he should stick it into the firkin. When he did that, the butter all dried up and disappeared.

He went back to the king with the slice of bread in his hand and said, 'Do you want me to eat dry bread? There was not enough butter to cover it!'

The witch also helped him to tan the hides, and the second task was passed.

Then it was time to get the spancil off the cow. It turned out that the king's daughter had the spancil off the cow, and she was up in a high tower of the castle. The boy could hear her singing and followed the sound of her voice. When he climbed up the wall and jumped through the window, there she was with her father. The boy asked her for the spancil. She refused to give it to him and instead threw it towards her father, but her throw went crooked and it was the boy that caught it. Her father cursed the woman for her poor throw, and from that day forward all women of that blood line have a crooked throw!

The triumphant boy had succeeded in all three tasks and could claim his prize. So Lon Mac Liofa got his cow back again, the marvellous cow whose milk would fill any vessel.

One day, a jealous woman bet Lon Mac Liofa that she had a vessel that the cow could not fill. 'Go ahead,' said the smith, and the cow was brought to the woman's place. She sat herself down on her stool and began to milk the beast into a milk strainer. The generous cow's milk flowed freely, spilling through the holes of the strainer and overflowing, running over the ground. The poor cow just kept going, until her heart burst open with grief and she fell down and died of a broken heart. Where the milk of the Glas Gaibreac ran over the ground, it turned to clear water and became a river that is still to be seen there today near Carron, known as the Seven Streams of Taosca. Some people say that the water of the Seven Streams has healing power.

They say the spot where the cow died can still be seen, as not a single blade of grass ever grew there since, while the beds where the cow rested are called 'Leaba na Glaise' and are bright green patches in the grey limestone rock.

References:
SFS (1937-38) John Costelloe, Coad told to Maire ni Costelloe; Sean Mac Eoin; *Folklore of Clare*, T.J. Westropp (Clasp Press; Ennis, 2000)

4

MERMAIDS, SWAN MAIDENS & OTHER SHAPESHIFTERS

CONOR O'QUIN AND THE SWAN MAIDEN

There was a young chief, Conor O'Quin, who lived near Inchiquin Lake. One day, as he was out walking near an old stone fort by the lake, he saw a large number of swans swimming on the water, heading in towards the southern shore. As he watched them, the swans stretched their necks, shook out their wings and walked ashore. There they seemed to grow taller and, removing black hoods and feathered dresses, they became a group of graceful young women dressed in thin white shifts. These girls danced and chattered there at the lake's reedy edge. One girl sat on a rock to comb her black hair, and turned her face in O'Quin's direction.

O'Quin had never seen such a beauty before, and he was immediately smitten. The girl, when she noticed the man watching her, took up her feathered dress and flew off over the water, the other swan-girls behind her in graceful flight.

O'Quin could not get the face of this beautiful swan
maiden from his mind. He took to wandering down by the
lake each day in the hope of seeing her again. Three times he
caught a glimpse of her as she sat on the rock by the water's
edge combing her dark hair. Each time he approached she
would quickly pull on her hood and feathered dress and
take flight.

One day, however, O'Quin, now consumed with love for
the swan maiden, had a plan. He rose early and hid himself
behind some scrubby trees and bushes near the water's edge

and waited for the swans to come to shore. When they did, he watched them shake off their feathered dresses and hoods, biding his time, waiting only for the right moment to make his move. As his beloved lay down her black hood, O'Quin quickly grabbed it up and held it fast. This time the swan maiden could not escape him.

He asked her to marry him and come live with him in his grand house.

She tried to dissuade him. 'You would be better to marry one of your own kind,' she said. But O'Quin would not be put off. He asked again, stressing the depth of his love for her. At last she agreed to become his wife, but she named three conditions to her consent. The first condition was that the marriage must remain a secret; the second, that he must never invite an O'Brien into their house; and third, that he must not engage in games of chance.

O'Quin agreed at once, and swore that he would tell no one about his lovely bride; that he would never invite an O'Brien to the house; and that he would neither gamble nor play cards. He thought these conditions a small price to pay for the love of his life.

O'Quin scooped her up into his arms and carried her back to the grand house. There they lived happily together for many years. As time went by two children were born, and as they grew, all seemed well in the world for Conor O'Quin.

One day, O'Brien of Leamanagh and some of the other chiefs of the area decided to hold a tournament nearby at Coad. There would be horseraces, and great sport was promised. O'Quin's wife begged him not to go, but when he insisted, she pleaded with him to accept no invitation to dine, nor to invite anyone to dine at their house. O'Quin gave her his solemn word and set off for the races at Coad.

In the excitement of the day, he quite forgot his promise. He invited O'Brien to dine with him, and the chief came with all his retinue to O'Quin's house. O'Quin's wife prepared a glorious feast and served it up on the finest of dishes, but she spoke not one word. While O'Brien and his party ate their fill, entertained by her foolish husband, she took up her swan gown and put it on, along with her black hood. She carried her children, one under each arm, from their beds, and then slipped away down to the shores of the lake, and was never seen again in human form.

Not knowing about his loss, O'Quin played cards with O'Brien after dinner. He wagered his house and lands, and lost it all to Tadg O'Brien of Coad. O'Quin was a ruined man. Having broken his promises, he had lost all that he held dear: his wife, family, house and lands, all gone in one foolish, thoughtless night. They say O'Brien gave him a place to build a small house and he lived out his days there, a sad and broken man.

His spirit can still be seen to this day, wandering the shore on Lake Inchiquin in the hope that his beloved swan maiden might one day return.

THE NEWHALL MERMAID'S CURSE

A wealthy man named O'Brien lived in Newhall House. Nearby was a lake, at the foot of a long tree-covered hill, where O'Brien spent much of his time fishing. The local peasants told O'Brien that a mermaid lived in that lake. They had seen her wearing a green cloak, sitting on a rock at the lake's edge, combing her long black hair. O'Brien laughed at their foolish stories. He was very rich and cared little for the poor people who lived around him. All that concerned him was sport and making money. His house was very grand. There were marble pillars by the heavy carved wooden doors, and tall windows that let in plenty of light to his drawing room. And the furniture, well there were chairs there with legs painted gold and covered in brocade cushions. He kept a number of servants, none of whom he treated well. He was known as a cruel master, and no one would want to cross him.

Underneath his grand mansion there was a cellar, where he kept his store of fine wines. When he had company he wished to impress, he would send a servant down to bring up a bottle or two of some particularly fine vintage. At other times he would go down to the cellar himself to admire his store. It was not particularly pleasant in the cellar, being cold and damp and with a constant sound of running water – some said an underground stream ran beneath it.

One day, O'Brien noticed that some of his wine was missing. He presumed that his servant had stolen it, and made up his mind to prosecute the man. As he would need evidence, O'Brien decided to stay up that night to catch the thief red-handed.

He dressed warmly and made himself as comfortable as he could, using an old wine cask as a chair, and he waited.

Just after midnight he heard movement at the far end of the cellar. He was greatly surprised when he saw the thief: it was a woman, of sorts, above the waist, but with scales and a tail like a fish below. The mermaid came from Newhall Lake, along the narrow covered stream that ran from under the cellar to the lake.

O'Brien had never seen such a creature before; he had thought the tales of mermaids in the nearby lake to be just the foolishness and superstition of the peasantry. O'Brien, who had his pistol ready to confront the thief, fired at the mermaid and his shot wounded her badly. She gave an ear-shattering shriek that echoed all around the cellar. Before she disappeared, bleeding, along the channel to the lake, the mermaid cursed the O'Briens that they would never have an heir.

'Fish without flesh, meat without bones, hear the mermaid's curse on the plains of Killone.

As the mermaid floats bloodless down the stream, so shall the O'Briens pass away from Killone.'

The mermaid's curse proved to be true, and this was how it worked out. O'Brien had seven daughters and no sons. One of the daughters married a man called McDonnell and they had seven daughters too.

The wounded mermaid floated back to the lake, which turned red with her blood for a day and a night. It is said that it still turns red once every seven years. And it will turn red if an O'Brien should be in residence at Newhall House. Cattle will not drink from the lake when it is red with the mermaid's blood.

The mermaid also said that a crow would never build its nest or live in the wood near Newhall House after that day, and this also came to pass.

STOLEN BUTTER

Major Moloney was a landlord who lived at Kiltannon, over near O'Callaghan's Mills. His lands were broad and spread over a large part of East Clare. A man called James Hanlon paid rent to the Major for a small farm at Corraclune, near Clonusker. James kept a herd of black and white cows, but although the cows were still giving milk, and it looked as creamy as ever it had, he had been unable to make any butter for the last month or so. It just would not churn.

At first he paid no heed to it, thinking, well, don't we all have a bad day some time? But when the same thing happened every time he went to make butter, he knew there was something wrong. He started to remember what his old auntie used to say about people who would stole butter. What was it? If someone took water from your well before yourself on May morning they'd have your butter for the year. Was that it? He knew his auntie used to bring in a whitethorn branch to the house on May Eve to bring luck for the year. He used to think it was all just superstition, but now he was getting poorer all the time with no butter to sell. James decided he'd best go and ask Biddy Early for her advice on what to do. She would know if it was anything to do with fairies or magic, wouldn't she? Biddy lived over the other side of Feakle, so James set off one morning to her house. When he reached the door, Biddy was there to greet him, 'Well, hello and welcome, James Hanlon and God bless you. It'll be about the butter is it?'

James was not at all surprised that Biddy already knew the reason for his visit. After all, everyone in East Clare knew about Biddy's gift for healing and her blue bottle that showed her the future. Biddy brought James into the house, sat him down and made him some tea. She listened as James told his story, describing how he couldn't make the butter at all. Then she told him, 'There is an old woman, a witch, who stole your butter on May morning, by turning herself into a hare. She will try to do it again next May morning, and you will get no butter until you catch and stop her. The only thing that can stop her is a black hound with not a rib of white hair on it.'

James went home, wondering how he would get this black hound with no white on it, when he had hardly a penny left to his name. He went to see the landlord and told him what Biddy had said. Major Moloney was a wealthy man, and he agreed that he would pay for the hound. The Major sent out word all over the country that he was looking for a black hound with no rib of white hair, but no one in Ireland had such a hound. He sent then to Scotland, but they too had no such hound. At last he found a black

hound with no rib of white hair in England. The Major paid 100 English pounds for the beast, and had him shipped over on the boat. He was a fine looking beast, smooth and sleek, and not a single white hair on him. The Major trained the hound himself to be ready for the following May Day and the hound proved to be fast and a great hunter.

On May Eve, all of John's friends gathered at his house. They brought all the cows into a little paddock next to the house, where they could keep an eye on them. Early next morning, before the sun was up, the Major's men brought the hound to James' house. As the sun rose over the horizon, James had the hound on a long leash, and his friends all watching for the hare. They were only just out the door when the hare came bounding into the paddock where all the cows were lying on the grass. The hare went to the first cow and began to suck on its teats. When she'd taken her fill, the hare moved on to the next cow. She went from one cow to the next, drinking the milk from each in turn.

James unfastened the leash and let the hound free. The Major had trained him well. As soon as he caught sight and scent of the hare, he was off, and a fine chase there was, like nothing ever seen before. The hare ran off up the mountain, with the black hound following close at her heels. The hare ran through fields and over bogs, across moorland and through scrubby trees, jumping over streams and splashing through rivers, and right behind her was the sleek black hound, who would give her no rest. When they had run 10 miles or more, the hare was beginning to tire. She knew she could not go further, so she turned for home. When they were close to Corraclune, the hare made a dash for a little mean-looking cottage. The hound was closer behind now, and the hare looked to be in a panic, trying to find the way into the house. The doors were closed, what was she to do? She saw that one window had a small pane of glass broken. The hare leapt for it, meaning to get in through that small window. Just as she leapt, the hound caught her back leg and bit her. The hare squealed with pain, struggling to get away. At last she got free and disappeared through the window.

The men who had followed the hunt opened the cottage door. The house was sparsely furnished, just a table and chair in the room by the fire. There was no sign of a hare. In another room there was an old woman in bed, groaning. 'What are ye after here?' she called out to the men. 'Can a sick old woman not get some peace in her own home?'

'Did you see a hare come in the house, Granny?' asked one of the men.

'I saw no hare. I am sick in my bed, I tell ye,' and she groaned again.

The men searched all around the room. 'Would you look at this!' said one, pointing to a trail of blood that ran from the broken window and across the floor to the bed where the old woman lay groaning in pain.

The black hound was brought back to James' farm, but when it reached the paddock it fell down dead. They buried it in the paddock and placed a carved stone over his grave.

James Hanlon had no further trouble making butter after that day.

THE TWO BROTHERS

There were two brothers, Francis and John, who lived together in a small house in the west of Clare. The day came when Francis had to leave home in search of his fortune. That morning he took his brother John down to a spring well near their home. As the two looked down at the clear water bubbling up into the pool, Francis told his brother that he should come to the well every day, for here he would find news. If the water in the pool should turn red, then he would know that Francis had died on his travels. The brothers shook hands, said their farewells, and Francis rode off into the wide world with his horse, his dog and his gun.

After a day or two Francis came to a cottage where a blacksmith lived. He asked for work, but the blacksmith had no work for him. He rode on to a big old mansion, and the people there gave him a task. He was to kill a hare that was stealing the milk from their cows. Francis rose early next morning and set out with his horse, his dog and his gun. When he got out to the field where they kept their cattle, he saw the hare milking the cows. Francis fired a shot at the hare, but did not kill her. The wounded hare bounded unsteadily away. Francis followed the hare to a ramshackle hut and watched it disappear through a crack in the wall. When he opened the door, he saw no hare inside, only an old woman lying moaning in the corner.

'Are ye alright there, old woman?' asked Francis. His dog began to growl and pace nervously.

There was a bone on the floor near the old woman. 'Oh I am fine, son,' she says. 'That's a grand dog you have there. Why don't you give it the bone?'

Francis gave his dog the bone. As soon as it began to chew, its paws suddenly became stuck to the floor and the dog could not move an inch.

'That's a fine horse you have. Why don't you feed it some oats?' said the old woman, pointing towards a bag of oats by the wall.

Francis brought the oats to his horse, and as soon as the horse put its nose into the bag, its feet were stuck to the ground.

Francis began to wonder if the old woman was a witch, but before he could stop her, the old woman leapt up and killed him with an axe.

The next day, back at the small house in the west of Clare, John went to the well for water. What he saw filled his heart with grief, for the water was red and he knew his brother was dead. John decided he would travel out into the world himself, and see could he find where his brother was buried. Sure, what else could he do?

He made ready his horse, called his dog, and took up his gun, and off he rode into the wide world. After some time he came to a blacksmith's forge. He asked for work there, but the smith had no work for him. He rode on and came to a big old mansion, and he got work there. He was out in the field next morning when he saw a hare stealing milk from the cow. He fired a shot at her and wounded her. John followed the limping hare to a ramshackle hut and watched her disappear through a crack in the wall. When he opened the door, he saw no hare inside, only an old woman lying moaning in the corner. His dog began to growl and pace nervously.

'Are ye alright there, old woman?' asked John.

'Oh I am fine, son,' she says, 'but that's a grand dog you have there. Maybe it would like a bone?' She pointed to the bone on the floor.

John shook his head, 'My dog has eaten well this morning already.'

'That's a fine horse you have. Maybe it would want some oats?' The old woman pointed towards a bag of oats by the wall.

John shook his head, 'My horse has eaten well this morning already.'

The old woman got up unsteadily, and she commanded the dog, 'Dog, help me!' But the dog just growled, bared its teeth and leapt at her with his claws out.

'Horse, help me!' she cried, but the horse only reared and kicked out at her.

John spoke then, 'I know who you are, old woman, and I believe that you are responsible for my brother's death.'

She knew then that she was found out, and feared she would be killed. The old woman pleaded for her life, 'Spare me, and I will give your brother back to you, and I swear, I will never again cause harm to anyone!'

When John agreed, his dear brother Francis was instantly restored to him, none the worse for his short journey to the land of the dead. The old woman kept her word and never stole milk again. In fact she became a model of virtue in the world, doing what good she could for everyone she met thereafter.

The two brothers celebrated their good fortune, then set off together on the road, and no doubt they found many further adventures. For all I know they may be travelling still, if the roads have not turned to gold and the stars fallen silver on the fields.

HEARTS OF STONE

There were three wealthy brothers who lived near Classagh Hill. They lived in a big house and they had many acres of good land. Their land was dark and rich and gave them plentiful crops each year. They kept large flocks of sheep and cattle that provided them with plenty of meat and milk and plenty to trade. However, no matter how much they had, or how rich they grew, they worried constantly about losing their wealth, and so they were mean and miserly. If a beggar came to their door, they would send him on his way without so much as a crust of bread.

In those days, there was a monastery nearby. Every year at harvest time, the monks would send a friar out around the country to visit all the farms in the locality. Each farm would give a portion of their corn to the monks – that was how the monks made their living. The monks did all the praying, and the people on the farms supported them to do that, each giving a sieve of wheat to the monastery.

One year, when harvest time had come around again, a fresh-faced young friar arrived at the miserly brothers' barn door, a broad smile on his face and a sack almost full of wheat over his shoulder.

'Good morning to you gentlemen. I have come to claim the monks' share of your harvest: a sieve full of your finest corn. God bless you, workers of the land, for the bounty God gives.'

The three wealthy misers grumbled. 'Workers of the land, we are, but the bounty is our own!'

'Psah! It was our own sweat and back-breaking work that grew this corn.'

'Why do we owe any of our harvest to these pampered monks? What do they give to us? Nothing!' They went into the barn, still moaning, then one of the brothers had an idea. He took up the sieve and turned it in his hands. 'Look, brothers. The sieve has two sides to it: the bottom and the mouth,' he said.

'The monks did not say which side of the sieve we should fill. We can fill the bottom!'

The others clapped him on the back and laughed at how they could cheat the naive young friar and give him less of their wheat than he expected. They measured out a small amount of grain in the bottom of the sieve.

The young friar came into the barn and watched as they emptied the sieve into the sack. Something was not right, and the sack hardly looked any fuller at all.

'Are you sure you gave me the full sieve of wheat, my good brothers?' asked the friar.

'Oh yes, we did all right,' sniggered the brothers.

The young friar might have been naive but he could still tell they were trying to cheat him. He spread his arms, looked up to the heavens and spoke a curse upon them, 'May God turn you mean and unholy brothers to stone as hard as your hearts!'

The three misers froze where they stood. A dog that came running and barking at the friar was also turned to stone. Those three large stones and one small one are still standing on the hill to this day. The place is known as Knockfearbreag, the hill of the deceitful men.

References:

The Swan Maiden: *Irish Birds, Facts, Folklore and History*, Glynn Anderson (Collins Press, 2008); *Folklore of Clare*, T.J. Westropp's (Clasp Press; Ennis, 2000).

The Newhall Mermaid's Curse: SFS (1937-38) adapted from a story told to Brendan Walker by Lot Malone, Darragh, Baile Aoda, p.3.

Stolen Butter: SFS (1937-38) adapted from a story Eileen Guilfoyle heard from Michael Guilfoyle, Bridge St Scariff, Scariff p.69.

The Two Brothers: SFS (1937-38) Mary Nolan, heard from Mr Tom O'Dea, Clonina, Cree.

Hearts of Stone: SFS (1937-38) Daniel Sweeney, Clooney School, p.302.

5

HEROES

FIONN MAC CUMHALL

The summit of Slieve Callan or Mount Callan is the highest point in west Clare. Near to this summit, huge numbers of people gathered each year for the Lughnasadh celebrations in late July or early August. This was the time to celebrate the beginning of the harvest, to give thanks for nature's abundance, for girls and boys to pick fraughans (blueberries), and to decorate sacred wells with garlands of flowers. There would be games, sports, contests and feasting. Perhaps it was around Lughnasadh time that Fionn Mac Cumhall, the legendary hunter/warrior, was visiting this part of the world.

While Fionn was down in this area with a large party of his Fianna, his band of warriors, he made himself a camp at the foot of Mount Callan. There was great hunting there, and Fionn had all that he could want. The only thing that was missing was a good and reliable personal servant.

One day, a small man dressed all in brown walked into Fionn's camp and presented himself to the bold warrior chief. This was a strange-looking character, just three feet tall, and wearing a three-cornered hat on his shaggy brown head. The little man strode into the camp, bold as anything, and demanded to be taken to Fionn, saying, 'I hear that the chief is in need of a personal servant. I wish to present myself for that position,' and he removed his hat and bowed. Amused, Fionn agreed and took the little man on as his servant.

We all know how the Fianna enjoyed their sport. When there were no battles to be fought they had races and athletics competitions to keep themselves fit and trim and ready for action. One day, while they were decamped at Mount Callan, they held a jumping contest, and all the bold warriors took it in turns to leap across the river at its broadest point. Grainne, Fionn's unwilling bride, was there too, and she was dressed in her finest to give out the prize to the winner.

The little brown man feared that Conan Moal was going to win the prize. Conan was getting ready, taking his first running steps towards the river's edge, and had just launched himself into the air when the little brown man threw his hat at him. Well, the distraction certainly put Conan off his leap. He twisted in the air, limbs all askew. The three-cornered hat struck him in the eye and Conan fell with a heavy and rather ungainly splash into the deep river. This was no graceful salmon's leap, in fact it was more like a large stone sinking. He was knocked unconscious by his fall and had to be carried out on a stretcher before he drowned in the cold water.

The druid doctor brought his smelling salts and rubbed Conan's feet and hands, and slapped his face till he regained consciousness.

Meanwhile, the little brown man, fearing retribution, ran for his life. He had bit of magic himself, and so he was able to become invisible, but only for a few minutes at a time. If you were watching, you'd see him suddenly appear in front of this tree or that boulder a few steps apart.

Now that he was back among the living, Conan was furious with the little man. He pulled up a bunch of herbs, changed into a hawk and flew up into the air. The hawk soared overhead. He soon caught up with the little man at Dun Sallagh, and brought him back to Fionn's camp. He was put on trial for seditious behaviour, betrayal of trust and throwing his hat at a competitor in an otherwise fair contest, and he was found guilty as charged. Fionn sentenced him to stand guard on the height of Mount Callan until a small lake that was there should run dry. He will be there still to this day, keeping his watch over the lake, which has never been known to dry up.

If you have a reason to pass by the Hand Cross Roads, you had best beware, for people say that the little brown man meets unwary travellers on the road and sets them astray.

FIONN RESCUES A BABY

One day, when Fionn Mac Cumhal was out hunting in the Burren hills, he became separated from his companions. Brave warrior that he was, he was not concerned and after a while he found himself by the village of Ballyvaughan. He was just enjoying a game of hurling by the shore when a boat came into the harbour. The men on board ran straight to Fionn, saying that their queen had urgent need of his help. Never one to refuse a lady in distress, Fionn went with them at once. They were several days at sea before they landed near the Queen's house. She greeted Fionn and explained that a witch was going to take her only child that night.

Fionn agreed to keep watch over the child as it slept that night, but after supper Fionn felt himself grow weary. It was a spell the witch had placed upon him, and he was powerless to fight it. He fell into a deep sleep. When he awoke, the child was gone and the men were arming themselves and making ready to pursue the witch.

They could see the faint eerie light of the witch's boat a long way off. They set sail and followed it. At last, they came to an island where they saw a revolving tower. One of the men spoke some words, commanding the tower to stop turning, and Fionn was able to climb to the top. There he found the witch asleep on the floor and the child in her arms.

Fionn gently lifted the child from the witch's arms and brought her to the ship and they set off again. But they had not been sailing for long before they saw the eerie light of the witch's boat behind them. Her boat was steadily drawing nearer, and so Fionn brought out his bow and arrow, took careful aim, and shot the witch through the heart.

Fionn carried the child back to the queen, who was anxiously waiting.

DIARMID AND GRAINNE

When Fionn was an elderly man, and had been without a wife for several years, he got engaged to Grainne, daughter of the King of Tara. The wedding was all prepared, but just before the feast Grainne chanced to see one of Fionn's men, a handsome young fellow named Diarmid. Grainne was lost; she fell in love with him instantly and begged him to come away with her. 'How can you let me marry that old man, when you are my true and only love?'

Diarmid, being a loyal follower of Fionn's, resisted Grainne's entreaties – but not for too long. He soon agreed that he loved her too, and the couple planned their elopement. Grainne slipped a sleeping potion into Fionn's wine and the lovers ran off together into the night.

When Fionn discovered this betrayal, he gathered the Fianna together and swore that they would pursue the couple relentlessly, until Grainne returned to him. He cursed them so that they would find no house in the whole land of Ireland that would give them a night's shelter or rest. All over the land of Ireland the couple fled, and wherever they went the Fianna followed close on their heels.

When Diarmid and Grainne reached County Clare they rested outside for a few hours here and there, on beds of stone that became known as Leaba Diarmid agus Grianne – Diarmid and Grainne's Bed. There is a dolmen by the side of the road to Miltown Malbay, just past the Hand Crossroads, that is one of Diarmid and Grainne's Beds. It is said that when the couple were on the run they had leapt over from Kerry, bringing the huge stones with them; Diarmid carrying the two massive upright stones under his arms and Grainne carrying the roof slab in her apron. Such a desperate obsessive love they must have had, that they still ran on, despite the hardship of never having a good night's sleep.

The lovers rested for a while in a cave at the foot of a cliff in Lismulbreeda. They must have lived there for some time for they made it as homely as they could. There are rocks there that seem like a table and chairs and another bed, while other stones were their candlesticks. People say there was a subterranean tunnel that leads from the cave to a dolmen at Mount Callan, known as Altar na Grianne.

They were by the western shore when Diarmid had an inspired notion. He remembered that Fionn could always tell where Grainne lay by biting on his magical oracular thumb (how he came by that is a whole other story altogether!). This was how Fionn had been able to follow their movements so closely. Now Diarmid gathered seaweed from the below the tideline and Grainne helped him spread it like a blanket over the stone bed. Diarmid hoped that the images Fionn would see now – Grainne resting beneath seaweed – would surely make him think the pair had drowned and lay beneath the waves. Perhaps it worked, or at least it bought them time, for at last an uneasy truce was called.

BRIAN BORU AND AOIBHEALL THE BANSHEE

In the time of Brian Boru, High King of Ireland, there lived, on a craggy hilltop above the shore of Lough Derg, a woman of the Sidhe by the name of Aiobheall. Long before that time she had been known as Aoibheann the Lovely One, a queen and protective spirit of the land and its sovereignty. Her home was on Slieve Bearnagh, and her name is found on landscape features that carry echoes of her presence even today on the slopes above the lough near Killaloe.

There is a high crag, Carrickeevul, up at the top of Crag Hill, surrounded by forest, where Aoibheall used to sit to keep a watchful eye over the Shannon River and the lands beyond. From here she could command the weather, brewing up storms and high winds when needed to protect her people. She had two spring wells on the lower slopes of Crag Hill. One was her clean well, for washing her hands and face, the other was her dirty well, where she washed her feet. One of these, called Tobereevul, still flows from under a rock on the side of the hill below her seat at Craglea, but I couldn't tell you whether it is the clean or the dirty well.

As time went on, Aoibheall the lovely, powerful spirit of the land, became somewhat diminished in the people's imaginations. She became known as the banshee of the Dal gCais clan. In this role, she was a guiding force to Brian Boru, as he rose from local chief to became the first Ard Ri, or high king, uniting the Irish clans against the Vikings.

It was the year 1014, and Murragh, the eldest son of Brian Boru, was at the palace of Kincora in Killaloe, preparing for the long journey to Dublin, to join his father's army against the Viking forces. Aoibheall came to Murragh just before he set off and delivered this warning, 'If you should meet a red-haired woman before you cross the Bow River (between Scariff and Mountshannon), then you will die in the battle.'

As Murragh's men reached the small river that once marked the boundary between Clare and Galway, they did indeed meet a red-haired woman.

Whilst the Battle of Clontarf raged, Brian Boru's army faced Vikings from Dublin, reinforced by armies from Iceland and the Orkney Isles. It was the night before Good Friday when Aoibheall came to Brian. She appeared to him like a vision, surrounded by glowing light, truly Aiobheall the Lovely One, to warn him: 'Brian Boru, King of the Irish you may be today, but tomorrow you will lie equal to all the other dead on the field of battle.'

Brian had lived a long and eventful life, and now, aged seventy-three, was ready to face this moment. 'If victory to the Irish is assured tomorrow, then my own life is a small price to pay for it. So be it.'

Next morning, a page brought news that Brian's son Murragh had fallen in the battle, and he begged Brian to retreat to his camp. Brian refused to hear of it, insisting, 'We will not retreat! What need is there, when I know that I myself will meet my death today on the field of battle. Aoibheall, the banshee of Craglea, came to me last night and told me so. I cannot escape her word, so I will fight today, and die in glory. May victory be ours!'

Aoibheall's warning came to pass. As he knelt in prayer in his tent, Brian Boru was slain on Good Friday 1014.

BRIAN BORU AND THE DANES' FORT

One time, when Brian Boru was down in west Clare, he went to Scattery Island, then on to Kilrush, up through Cooraclare and there he left his army behind him. He travelled on, on a secret mission, with just one soldier accompanying him to Cahermurphy, where the Danes were camped. He wanted to examine the Danes' defences and see how they could be breached. When he reached the camp, the fortress gates were locked. Brian saw that the fort could not be taken by force, but only if the gates were opened from the inside with a key

As Brian rode near to a hut, he heard a woman sobbing her heart out. He went closer and saw it was a young woman, and that she cradled a sickly baby in her arms. Both mother and child were gaunt and looked tired and hungry.

Brian asked her, 'Why are you crying so bitterly, woman?'

She told Brian, 'My husband is a Dane. He is a good enough man, but we are all hungry these days. I have no food to cook for him, and he said, he said …' The woman broke into a new fit of crying, 'He said that he will kill the baby and that I must cook it for his dinner if I have no food for him!'

Brian gave the woman some food from his own store. As her sobbing eased, the woman asked him, 'Tell me your name. I want to know, who is my benefactor?'

He told her that he was Brian Boru. The grateful woman's eyes opened wide with surprise. 'So what brings you to the Danes' fort at Cahermurphy, Brian Boru?'

Brian told her that his business there was to find a way into the fortress, and that he could see the gates needed to open from within, with a key.

'My own husband is the gatekeeper! He keeps the key inside his shirt.' The woman, glad to be able to repay

Brian's kindness, said, 'I will put herbs in my husband's food to make him sick, and then I can get the key. I will open the gates and let you into the fort tonight when all the Danes are sleeping.'

That night, the woman did just as she had said. She opened the gates and Brian, with his companion, got into the fort. They killed all the Dane soldiers as they slept.

The only ones they did not kill were the chief of the Danes and his three sons. They saved them because the chief had a secret recipe for making a drink like whiskey out of the heather that grew on the mountain. Brian, as well as everyone else, wanted to know how the Danes made this excellent drink.

He asked the Danes over and over again, but none of them would give the recipe for the heather drink. It was a long interrogation, but at last the sons gave in and said that they would tell. The chief grew angry that his sons were willing to give the secret away. He looked at his sons crossly, and said to Brian, 'Do not listen to them! My sons don't know the whole process for making the drink. They have only ever helped me with certain parts of the process. They can't give you the recipe, for they do not know it all.'

Brian looked from the chief to his sons and considered what he had just heard. The chief continued, 'My sons have shown themselves unworthy of my name. I disown them. They are no longer my sons! It is best that you kill these cowards now. If you do, I will give you the recipe for the heather drink.'

The crafty chief thought he would be able to make his getaway while Brian and his men were busy killing the sons.

Brian gave the order and the three sons were put to death. Then Brian turned to the chief, who had not got far away, and asked again for the recipe.

'Hah! Did you really think I would tell you? I would rather lose my own life than give you the secret of making the heather drink. I will take the recipe with me to my grave!'

Brian's men killed the chief and buried all four brave men under a mound of stones near Cahermurphy South, now called Tullain a Madra.

References:

Fionn Mac Cumhall: SFS (1937-38) John Joe Shannon, Cregan Bui, Corofin, from his father; SFS (1937-38) Miceal de Brucs, Scoil na mBrathar, Ennis, p.210.

Brian Boru: SFS (1937-38) Teresa Galvin from her grandmother; SFS (1937-38) P.J. Montgomery, Doonagan, was told this by John Donlan, reel 180.

6

FAIRIES

MAGGIE MALONE

There was once an old woman named Maggie Malone, who lived around Ballycar long ago. She had one leg shorter than the other, and an arm that was wasted and shrunken due to a childhood illness. When she was young, Maggie was what they used to call 'delicate'. Because of her condition, her parents kept Maggie in a cradle for her first seven years. At times she could neither talk nor walk and was hardly conscious, but seemed to move in and out of a comatose state. The neighbours said the child was 'with the fairies' at these times, because whenever she recovered she would tell them strange tales of her experiences.

According to her stories, Maggie spent her times away riding on a grey horse. She said that she had spent the night riding in the company of many other horsemen and women with a pack of hounds in pursuit of a stray horse over the fields and forests around the whole parish. When they came to ditches, the splendid horses leapt them with ease. It was the same with hedges and rivers: no hedge was too tall, no river too broad. It seemed that nothing could prevent the party from their pursuit. The chase continued all through the night until the dawn. When the sun rose in the sky, the hounds and horses disappeared at once, and Maggie found herself back in her cradle, gazing at the ceiling with a dribble of spit at her lips. Every night it was the same: riding with the hunt all night, back in the cradle at daybreak.

Maggie could describe in detail the features of the members of the hunt who accompanied her each night of the chase. From her descriptions of the faces – a distinctively large nose, twisted mouth, or grey bushy eyebrows – and how they dressed, or carried themselves, her neighbours were able to recognise local people they had known, who were now long dead.

One night, as Maggie rode with the hunt, they came upon a party of men who carried a small coffin on their shoulders. Maggie and the hunt joined the funeral procession, and rode in a quiet and serious manner until they came to a farmer's house.

Outside the house the men laid the small coffin on the ground and removed the lid. Inside was a skinny, pale and delicate child. One man lifted the delicate child from the coffin and brought her to the window of the house. As Maggie watched, the window opened, seemingly of its own accord, as they drew near. Hands reached out towards them from the window, bearing the body of a beautiful child. The men gently took the beautiful child and handed over in exchange the delicate child. The exchange complete, the beautiful child was placed in the coffin, the lid replaced, and the funeral march began.

Now Maggie could see that there were only three men carrying the coffin, and they seemed to stumble under its weight. As the procession made its way towards Rinn na bFear Cross they came across a man fast asleep by the roadside, no doubt sleeping off his evening's visit to his neighbour. The men shook him awake and commanded him to help them. The man, white with fear, shook as he did as they said, and took up the fourth corner of the coffin. The procession continued along its way, until suddenly in a moment, the whole funeral party disappeared. The awakened sleeper found himself carrying the coffin alone.

He struggled on with it until he came to the very next house along the road. Here he tried to bring the coffin into the house, but the occupants would not let him in, saying, 'We have grief enough in this house!' Nonetheless he put down the coffin outside in their yard, and asked their help to open it up. None of them knew what they would find inside, and curiosity got the better of them, so they agreed. Prising off the coffin lid, they found inside their own young daughter, who had died a few days previously and been buried just the day before. Here she was, safe and well, rubbing her eyes as if she had just awoken from a long sleep.

Maggie claimed that the other child remained in a cradle for twenty-one years, and was always delicate and thin. Eventually she wasted away and died, but as long as she lived, the people of that house knew only good fortune, their animals prospered and no ill luck came near them.

THE FAIRIES' DANCE IN GLANDREE

Between the villages of Feakle and Tulla sits the lovely glen known as Glandree. Some would tell you that the name means 'valley of the druids', others say it is 'valley of enchantment'. But yet again, it may be named for the fairy folk who lived there, and some would say that dwell there still.

I lived there myself for a short while, when my son was just a toddler. Staying in a house without running water, we each day collected water from the stream that ran past the house for the washing, and brought drinking water from a spring in the field across the road. We hung the washing on the hedge or the bars of the gate to dry in the sunshine of that Indian summer. The bohereens were bordered with rough stone walls, framed by the bright fiery oranges and reds of montbretia and fuchsia and the creamy lace of meadowsweet. My few months in Glandree were a magical time in my life: a time of in-betweens. The end of summer, the beginning of a new way of living. I was there to take respite, to lick my wounds and prepare for life as a single parent. Life with a young child was simple, and it was magical, as I have found it always is, in those strange gaps in life when the everyday and the otherworld seem closer than usual. Fairies seemed to be there in abundance, and they are never far away when I visit friends who live there now.

Here is a story about two lads who lived in Glandree long ago:

There lived in Glandree two boys, John Maher and Tim Clune. In their early days going to school, they were fast friends. As they grew to become young men they learned to sing and dance and play music. They were known as the sport of the place and were invited to all the big dances.

After a while, Tim got married to Mary, a lovely handsome girl, and the young couple settled down in a little house in Glandree. Sadly, Tim's young wife died just one year later, which brought a cloud of sorrow and gloom on the place. Now there was no more fun or dances for poor Tim. His good friend John called round often and tried to bring him some cheer, but to no avail. Tim no longer had interest in cards, or music or sporting. By the time another year had passed John got sick himself and before long he died. Now poor Tim was all alone, without his wife and his closest friend. He was a broken man, and wandered about the roads and fields aimlessly. No one could reach him, he kept his own company and had time for nobody, just lived alone in that fine little house.

Those were dark days for Tim, but there finally came a day when Tim took a strange notion, and went to Tulla to meet his old friends. They were happy to see him out and about and spending his time in company. They fetched out a bottle of poitín, and Tim drowned his grief for that one day with a glass or two.

Later, as he was coming home, just as the night was growing dark, Tim took a short cut home, by what was known as Helly's Fort. Just as he was about to climb over the stile, there he met his old friend John, standing as if he'd been waiting for Tim. Tim was afraid to see what must be the ghost of his old friend, and thought to run away.

But John called out to him 'Tim, I never did you any harm in life, nor will I now I am dead. If you come with me now I tell you, you will enjoy the best night you ever had in your life! Don't you remember the many good nights we had together?

Tim paused a while and pinched himself. If this was a ghost, it seemed friendly enough. He said, 'John, old friend, or spirit, or whatever you are, what do you plan to do with me?'

'I plan to cheer you up!' said John. 'Come with me tonight, and I swear I will leave you safe and sound in this same spot in the morning. Now Tim, you must agree to pass no remarks, nor ask any questions of anybody but me. You can ask me for anything you want, and I will give it to you.'

John took Tim by the hand, and together they walked a few steps from where they stood. The next he knew, Tim found himself in a beautiful building. It seemed like a fine big house, grander than any he had seen before. John brought him to a dining hall where the tables were laid out with fine damask cloths, and the plates and dishes were all of gold and silver. The tables were laden with all kinds of eating and drinking, and handsome young ladies dressed in the latest of fashions served around the table. Tim ate and drank whatever he fancied from the platters then sat back in his velvet chair, with his belly full and a warm sense of satisfaction.

John came to him then and led him through tall double doors into a dance hall, full of dancing couples. The whole room was moving together, leaping and bounding in grand style. John handed Tim a violin and took one up himself. They both played together for the next set in splendid style. As Tim's spirits rose higher he forgot his grief and sadness. 'Begor John,' said he, 'we will dance the next set!'

Next thing four lovely girls stepped out onto the floor. Two of them advanced towards Tim and John. One of them whispered to Tim and asked him to dance with her. Tim smiled, nodded and took her hand.

When the set was over, the fine young lady brought Tim back through to the dining hall, where he helped himself to more refreshments.

When he came back again to the ballroom Tim heard a small little man announcing another dance. 'Ladies and gentlemen, get ready for the polka'. Now all the young folk in the hall got up and began to dance together, passing each other hand to hand in a weaving line. As they were

exchanging partners, who should jump into Tim's arms but his own dead wife, Mary. She looked as handsome as she ever had, in a lovely cream dress with green ribbons, and with fine pink roses in her cheeks from the dancing.

'Oh my sweet holy God! Mary, is it really you?' Tim asked her, forgetting that his friend had warned him to speak to no one but himself.

Just as he spoke the words, the music and the dancing stopped dead. He heard the small man say, 'Tim, you must let her go now.'

Tim, having just that moment found her again, got excited and shouted, 'Mary I will hold you, come whatever will. Dead or alive, I will not let you go!'

Suddenly all the beautiful lights and colours faded to nothing, and the whole grand building seemed to crumble and fall away like dust. Poor Tim's head was spinning and reeling as the stars seemed to dance around him in circles until he was dizzy and faint. His poor soul could bear the strain no longer.

The next thing he knew he found himself standing at the stile where he had met John. It was now mid-morning and the sun was high in the sky. When he reached home, Tim thought to take down his fiddle from the high shelf where it had sat for the past three years and began to rosin the bow. It might be time to remember and play a tune or two.

THE TAKING OF PADDY'S HUMP

There was a man called Paddy Hegarty who lived in the townland of Glandree in East Clare about 100 years ago. Paddy was born with a deformed spine. It was all curved round itself and he ended up growing up with a hump on his back. When he was a child, his parents took him for cures and probably to Biddy Early herself, but all to no avail. He had to like it or lump it, and in this case, it was a big lump altogether.

Apart from his deformity, Paddy was a fine looking man, and smart with it. He had married an awfully nice woman and they had two lovely daughters, who were his pride and joy. He couldn't be happier with his lot. The only thing he would have wished was different, if he had a wish, was that the hump be gone from his back and he be able to stand up tall and proud.

Paddy lived in a nice house and owned a few acres of good land, divided up into small fields by rough stone walls. Paddy kept the place tidy and looked after his stock well. One of his fields edged onto an old fort, a circle of earthen bank with hawthorn bushes growing on it. Paddy remarked often that he heard music when he passed that fort, especially if he passed that way around midday, he was sure there was music in there, though he could not say for certain if it was pipes or fiddles or singing he was hearing.

One night, he was taking a stroll around the fields and just as he was passing the old fort he met a small man wearing a green cap. Paddy introduced himself and asked the little man what his name was, and the little fellow said, 'Monday.'

'That's a grand name,' said Paddy, 'and who is your father?'

The little man said, 'Tuesday.'

'And your mother's name?' asked Paddy.

'Wednesday,' said the little man.

When Paddy asked if he had any brothers and sisters, the small fellow nodded, saying he had a brother called Thursday. All of a sudden, the little man disappeared, and Paddy walked on home.

Paddy had just got back into his house when a splendid lady walked in. She was a lovely looking woman, dressed in a fine satin gown, and wearing gold in her ears and shining ruby and emerald jewels around her neck. Her yellow hair was piled up on top of her head, with little golden curls falling softly around her face. Paddy bowed before the grand lady and stretched out his hand to shake hers. All this time Paddy's wife and daughters had just got on with their usual tasks in the home, as if no grand lady had stepped in their door.

'Come here now,' said Paddy to his wife, 'and greet our honourable guest.' But though his wife wanted to please him, she could see no guest, grand or otherwise, and she could not pretend to see someone who was not there! She was wondering then, had Paddy lost his senses.

The grand lady asked Paddy, 'Do you know who I am?'

Paddy nodded, 'I do. You are Wednesday.'

The grand lady smiled at Paddy and laid a green jewelled purse on the table. Then she disappeared, just as suddenly as she had come. When he opened the purse, Paddy found a note saying the contents were to be divided between his wife and his daughters.

Well, they might not have seen the lady herself, but the purse was there on the table and was real enough. When Paddy emptied it onto the table, it was jewels that sparkled and shone. His wife and daughters were afraid to touch the jewels, thinking this was some fairy magic and best left alone. Paddy tried to persuade them that all would be well, but they would have nothing to do with the jewels. In the end Paddy put them in a little carved ivory box that he kept his treasures in, and locked it away in the dresser drawer.

That evening, when he had all the stock seen to and all his day's jobs done, Paddy went for a stroll around the fields, as was his habit. As he was passing by the old fort he could hear the music again. He sat down on a mossy root where he liked to take his ease of an evening and smoke his pipe. Now it sounded as if there were hundreds of voices all singing together, and the words of the song were clear to him. The words of the song were: 'Monday, Tuesday, Wednesday, Thursday.'

Paddy stood up, the melody still in his head. Without thinking at all, he sang out, 'Friday, Saturday, Sunday.'

Next thing he knew, there was the little man with the green cap, standing before him. The little man took the hump from off of Paddy's back, and then disappeared. Paddy stood there, tall and proud, just as he might have wished, if he'd had a wish. Just to be sure, he patted at his back, but it was definitely gone.

When he arrived home his wife looked at him strangely, and said, 'What did you do? What happened that the hump is gone?'

Paddy told her that the little man had taken the hump off his back. He said, 'If this is fairy magic, then there is no harm in it, and nothing but good for us. Go to the dresser, my dear, and get the jewels the good lady brought you. Put them on, you and the girls. Let us be glad for all they given us!'

So Paddy's wife and daughters put on the jewels and did they not look magnificent. When he was out and about, people noticed that Paddy had lost his hump and was now a fine figure of a man. Stories were spread about what had befallen him, and when people asked him outright, Paddy had no qualms telling them exactly as it had happened. That was how it was, and didn't he have the jewels to show, and the hump gone to prove it?

There was a Protestant bishop who had a hump every bit as large as Paddy's had been. He came to hear from Paddy how he had lost his hump. Paddy brought him to his house and his wife served the bishop tea and cake. Then Paddy told the bishop the truth of how it had happened.

The bishop said, 'I will go and sit in that same spot, and we will see will your fairies take my hump from me too.'

So out went the bishop that evening, and he sat on the mossy root where Paddy liked to take his ease after his day's work was done. He'd been sitting there deep in his thoughts for half an hour when he heard the chorus of a hundred voices coming from the old fort.

He heard the voices singing, 'Friday, Saturday, Sunday,' and before he could think, he sang out, 'Monday, Tuesday, Wednesday!'

Suddenly he heard a voice in the fort calling, 'Take out Paddy's hump and add it to the one on the bishop's back.'

The next thing the bishop knew, he was almost bent over double under the weight of the two humps on his back. He went home to his wife and told his sad story. She called him a stupid man, and what a public disgrace he was now. The unfortunate bishop was that way for the rest of his life.

A FAIRY GIFT

There was once a house by an enchanted lake near Tulla. It was an isolated spot and there were no other houses anywhere near it. One day, there was a wake in that house, and one of the boys was sent to an outhouse to get hay for a visitor's horse. When he got there it seemed to him that all the hay was on fire. It looked like fire, but it wasn't at all hot when he got near to it, so he reached in and pulled out some hay for the horse, and he did not get burned. He couldn't understand it, but he just got on with it and fed the horse.

A month later that boy went to his bed one night and next morning he couldn't get up. He hadn't the strength to rise, and he lay there and just refused to move. He stayed in his bed for seven years, which is the term of a fairy term. When that time was over, he stayed in his bed another seven years. That made it fourteen years, or two fairy terms of spell.

During that time he found that he was able to mend any broken farm implement in just a few seconds. Whatever the people brought to him, no matter how badly bent, twisted or broken, he could fix it quicker than they could look at him. As well as this remarkable gift, he suddenly gained a huge appetite. He would eat as much as five men and still be hungry for more. So there was a good and a bad side to the fairy spell.

At midnight each night, the 'coach a bower' used to come into the yard. This was a ghostly coach, with no horses pulling it, that would scare the living daylights out of any strong man that saw it. As soon as he heard it coming, his strength returned and the boy would try to get up out of the bed, wanting to leave with the coach. It took four strong men of his family to hold him down, otherwise he'd have been out the window after it. As soon as the coach was gone, however, the boy's strength went from him again and he fell back into the bed, exhausted and pale.

During the night, every night for those fourteen years, fairies dressed in white used to come and cry and moan outside the house. It was awful the noise of it, and it is a miracle the family got any sleep in all those years, with the coach a bower and the crying fairies. When fourteen years were passed, the fairies came that night, still dressed in white, but this time they were singing and dancing and laughing. The very next day, that boy got up out of his bed as well as ever he had been before the spell was on him. He went on to live to a good old age, and he could still mend any farm implement that was given him, even after he was back to himself again. That was the gift the fairies left him.

PAT O'LEARY AND MOUNTAIN MARY

There was once a young woman called Mary, who lived with her father in a house on the side of the mountain. She was a good-looking girl alright, and there were many young fellows from the slopes around who found her worth turning back to get a second look at. There was a young man from around Kilkishin, Pat O'Leary, who had his heart set on marrying the girl. Mary was fond of Pat, and the two often went walking together whenever there was the opportunity. Pat picked posies of wild flowers and memorised poems for her. He was besotted. He wanted nothing more than to see himself walking down the aisle with his darling Mountain Mary on his arm, and them setting up home together in the cottage he was already fixing up as a home for them.

One Sunday he cleaned himself up, put on a smart coat and went to speak to Mary's father.

The father dismissed him, 'I am afraid, Pat O'Leary, you have come too late with your proposal. My daughter is promised to another, an English gentleman who will keep her in fine style and comfort.'

The English gentleman had a big house and a stretch of good land below the mountain. He had seen the girl when he was conducting some business with Mary's father. She was a fine-looking girl, sturdy and smart, and he was needing a wife, so had asked permission to marry her.

Although she would rather marry Pat than the Englishman, Mary did not want to displease her father. What could she do? She met Pat down by the river and they spoke about their troubles. 'You know it is you I love, Pat O'Leary, but I must do as my father says. Oh, how I wish it were not so!'

As Mary sobbed, Pat dabbed away her tears with his handkerchief. When the crying subsided, they sat together in silence, with only the sound of the birds and the river's babbling to disturb them. Suddenly, Pat had an inspiration. 'There is a way! We can elope together. I will sell my cow at the fair in Tulla, and we can still be married.'

Mary was agreeable, and an assignation was made to meet by an old oak tree the night after the fair.

The day of the fair came soon enough. Mary gathered her few possessions into a shawl and wondered how she could possibly wait until the appointed hour.

Meanwhile, Pat was up early and driving his cow to the fair. The road he took to Tulla led him past Cullaun Lake.

The cow, for no known reason, took a sudden notion to leap across a stone wall into the field that stretched down to the lake. Pat vaulted over the wall, calling, 'Husha, husha, Come back, you mad creature!' The cow leapt and bucked, kicking up her heels, as Pat ran to catch up with her, waving his stick and calling out pleas and curses as she headed in the direction of the lake. Pat followed the cow, still hoping to turn her back towards the road and continue on to the fair in Tulla.

Before he knew it, Pat found himself in a beautiful demense. Flat green fields of rich grasslands stretched before and behind him, with tidy ditches and tall stately trees. Pat looked around him and shook his head as if he was clearing water from his eyes and ears, or waking up from a too-deep sleep. His cow was nowhere to be seen, and where was he anyway? All thoughts of the cow, the fair in Tulla, Mountain Mary, just vanished, drifting away like soft clouds of thistledown. He stood quite still then, wondering, bewildered, not knowing who he was nor where he was going.

A tall man in a black tail coat strode towards him and raised his hat. 'Good morning, sir,' said the gentleman, bowing to Pat, 'You are most welcome.'

'Um and er, a good day to you, too, sir,' said Pat uncertainly.

The tall gentleman indicated a smooth broad path and requested that Pat follow him. Pat felt no inclination to refuse, and set off behind the gentleman. His guide brought him across the smooth grassy lawns to a door into a walled garden. Behind the walls were fruit trees laden with rosy apples and swollen ripe plums and unknown fruits hung in heavy bunches from creepers and vines that clung to the masonry. Another door opened into a garden where flowers of gentle colours filled the air with sweet and subtle perfumes.

The path continued on through corridors of box hedges clipped to beautiful curves. The guide brought Pat to the door of a stately mansion. The door was more than ten feet tall, flanked by marble pillars, topped by carvings of strange animals. The door was opened and Pat was led inside.

He cast his eyes around the enormous chamber. On couches draped with furs and silks were ancient Irish chiefs, all talking and making merry, drinking from gilded horns. They called to Pat to join them, and he did so, sinking into the soft cushions and drinking their sweet-sour drink. Poets came and proclaimed the heroic deeds of the chiefs to cheers and requests for more. Storytellers told tales that brought tears to the eyes of the strongest men, gladdened their hearts and shook their bellies with laughter. Musicians played upon the harp and pipes, melodies that caught up the heart and carried it as a bird is carried by the currents of the air.

Pat was then brought through to another chamber, even more vast than the last. Here heroes enacted famous Irish battles of the past. He watched as Brian Boru and his sons fought the Danes at the Battle of Clontarf. The next scene played out the Siege of Athlone and then the Siege of Limerick. At this sight Pat himself was so enraged at the plight of the women, that he had to be restrained from attempting to assist them. When the scenes of battle faded and quiet was restored, Pat was led out of the chamber and down a series of curving staircases into a vault piled high with treasures. His eyes were wide with wonder at the sight of so many gold pieces. His guide smiled and told Pat he was welcome to take whatever he wanted. 'Take as much as you can carry. Take whatever you may need.'

Pat picked up handfuls of gold coins and tossed them in the air, laughing. The coins fell with the clear tinkling ringing sound of bells. Pat filled his pockets and his hat. When Pat looked up, he saw fishes swimming overhead. At this strange sight Pat realised that he was underneath the lake!

The guide noticed this and smiled, 'It is time to return to your own world, Pat O'Leary.'

He led Pat back to the stairs and climbed up with him to the top. There Pat walked out into the sunlit morning. The guide bowed low once more and bade Pat farewell, handing him a hazel stick, saying, 'Speak well of us, Pat O'Leary.'

'Farewell and thank you, sir. I have met nothing but kindness here, and have no fear to speak of it so,' said Pat, bowing to the tall gentleman who faded into the morning light.

Pat looked around. He saw his cow calmly grazing in the rich green field. The demense had vanished and he was once more standing in the field by the lake. It was still early morning, and he'd best be getting on to the fair in Tulla.

When he reached the fair, the people came up to greet him. One man said, 'Well now, stranger, where have ye been this past twelve months?' Another took his hand saying, 'Pat O'Leary, 'tis twelve months since we saw ye in Tulla. Where have ye been, man?'

A crowd gathered around him, all wanting to hear the news of his travels and adventures since he'd left a year ago. Pat thought he had only been gone the one night! Suddenly he thought of Mary, and he asked, 'Is Mountain Mary here at the fair? Where can I find her?'

The people told Pat that Mary was going to be married that very day to the English gentleman. 'Then I am not too late!' cried Pat, as he used his stick to clear a path through the crowd towards where Mary was standing.

He reached for her hand and knelt before her. 'Is it true? Are you marrying the Englishman?' Pat asked.

Mary looked down at her beloved Pat, and with tears clouding her eyes she said, 'Pat O'Leary! When you did not meet me by the tree that night one year past, I thought you had deserted me. I was mad with you then, but as time went on, I thought you must be dead! When my father wanted me to marry the Englishman, what else could I do? I swear I was so heartbroken, I could kill you now myself, if I was not so pleased to see you!'

'Will you marry me now, Mountain Mary?'

Of course Mountain Mary agreed, and the two were married that day.

The English gentleman found another mountain girl to marry sometime after, I believe.

It was only when they reached the cottage that Pat had been fixing up that he told his Mary about his strange adventure under Cullaun Lake. And it was only when he showed her the gold coins in his pockets that she knew he was speaking the truth. They were never short of money, and always happy together, as far as I have heard.

References:

Maggie Malone: SFS (1937-38) Maggie Malone, Quin, County Clare, Ballycar, p.216.

The Fairies Dance in Glandree: SFS (1937-38) Maire ni Maoloney, Glandree, Tulla. Drumcharley NS, p.176.

The Taking of Paddy's Hump: SFS (1937-38) Ref: Maire Maloney, Glendree, Tulla. Drumcharley NS, p.112.

A Fairy Gift: SFS (1937-38) Pat MacGrath, Knockjames, Tulla told to Denis Halpin, Kiltanon, Tulla. Tulla School p.97.

Pat O'Leary and Mountain Mary: Patrick Benson, Kilkishin, Kilkishin School, p.322.

7

GHOSTS &
THE DEAD

The Grateful Dead

There was a crossroad near Fanny O'Dea's pub in Lissycasey which was said to be haunted by a spirit. People were wary of reaching that crossroad after dark because they feared meeting the ghost.

There was a young man who had some potatoes to take to the market in Ennis. It was winter time, when the days are short, and because of one thing and another, he did not reach the town until early evening. Walking along the streets of Ennis, he met his neighbours, already on their way home after a day at the market.

The neighbours called to him, 'It is late enough to be starting out. What will you do when you come to the haunted crossroad? Are you not afraid to pass that spot alone, and in the dark?'

'I am not concerned,' said the young man brightly. 'The moon is full, I will be able to see my way, and I will most likely overtake you on my way home!'

Night came on quickly, sooner than he had expected, and the young man had some trouble to sell his potatoes. It was not until late into the night that he was able to start for home. He set off on his horse and cart on the road out of the town in the dark of night, with the moon for company, whistling as he went.

When he reached the spot where the spirit was known to dwell, there he saw a pale young woman dancing in the moonlight. She moved with grace and seemed to shimmer under the moon's glow. Not daunted, he leapt from his cart and began to dance opposite her. When she stopped dancing, he asked her, 'What is it, in the name of God, that troubles you? Why do you haunt this place?'

The dancer answered, 'In the seven years since the day I died, you are the first man who has dared to speak to me. You are surely the best man to have passed this way in seven years. And, since you have asked me plainly, I am bound to tell you what troubles me, and why I linger here.'

'Tell me, and if I can help you I will,' said the young man in reply.

'A poor woman in the town of Ennis made for me a fine dress. I had the dress, but I had not paid the price of it before I took sick and died, and I was buried wearing the dress. Will you go to my aunt and ask her to pay the price of it on my behalf? If that is done, then I will be free to go, and will be seen no more at this crossroads.'

'As soon as I get home, I will go to your aunt, and I promise you that if she does not pay it, I will do so myself. Good night to you, spirit, and may your soul find peace and happiness.'

The very next day, the young man made good his promise and saw that the bill was paid. The dressmaker was delighted, and the dancing spirit was never seen again at the crossroads.

SAVOURY FLANAGAN

A man named Michael Flanagan lived near Barefield, not far from Ennis. He was known in the area as a great hero. He got the name Savoury Flanagan because at one time he saved the life of a young girl who was stolen away and thought to be dead. Michael was a great man for going out on his cuaird: that was going out to visit the neighbours of an evening to play cards, share stories and chat – and maybe have a little drink or two by the fire. That was the entertainment the men had before the television, and how news got carried from house to house.

It was a mild night, still and with a thin silver crescent of moon in the dark sky, when Michael was walking home one night from his cuaird. He was passing along a narrow lane, lined by tall trees whose branches met high overhead like a tunnel, when he met three men about his own height, dressed sombrely and carrying a coffin on their shoulders. They looked a little awkward, so Michael said, 'You are all off balance there, gentlemen, with only the three of you while the coffin has four corners. Here, let me give you hand with it, and save your backs. It looks like you will be passing my own door anyway.'

Michael set himself to the task and walked along with the other men, sharing the weight of the coffin on their shoulders. He carried it as far as his own door, but said he would go no further unless he could see what was in the coffin. The men agreed, so they set the coffin down on the wall outside while Michael called his mother and warned her not to be alarmed, that they were bringing in a coffin.

His mother cleared the cloth and dishes off the table so they could put the coffin there, and then Michael unscrewed the lid.

Well, Michael and his mother gasped when they saw what was in it. It was a beautiful young girl, lying there, pale and grey but still just breathing, her face contorted in the last agonies of death.

Michael gently lifted the girl from the coffin, wrapped her in warm woollen blankets and laid her down into a chair by the fire. He let her sit there until the morning, keeping watch that the fire did not burn too low, adding another stick to keep it glowing and warm through the night. His mother lit the holy candle and kept it alight through the night with a prayer for the girl's soul. Just before the cock crowed and the sun began to tint the sky with red, a little colour returned to the girl's cheeks, and it seemed she would return to life again. Michael's mother made her weak sweet tea and helped her take small sips. When she was ready, she spoke a few words, 'I thank you for warming me and bringing me back to the land of the living. My home is in Croom in County Limerick. My own parents think that I am dead. In fact, they expect to bury me this day at one o'clock. If so much as a single shovel of earth is thrown onto my coffin, there will be no saving me. Can you help me?' she begged Michael, reaching for his hand with her own grey, bony fingers.

Michael placed a broom into the coffin and replaced the lid. He gave the coffin to the three men who had waited outside.

Pulling on his coat, Michael turned back to the girl. 'I have a fast horse,' he told her, 'and if I set off now, I can, I hope, reach the graveyard in time to save you.'

'Thank you,' said the girl, as she removed a golden ring from her finger and gave it to Michael. Her initials were engraved upon it. 'Take this, and give it to my brother. He will know it is mine.'

Michael leapt upon his horse and set off at a roaring gallop. He rode all morning and arrived at the graveyard just as the funeral party approached. The girl's family were standing, all dressed in black, by the side of the open grave, while the coffin was lying there, ready to be lowered into the earth.

Michael leapt from his sweating and lathered horse. 'Stop!' he cried. 'Do not lower the coffin, I beg you. Your daughter's life depends on it!'

The parents and the mourners thought Michael was a dangerous lunatic. 'How dare you disturb us at a time like this!' cried the girl's father. 'Seize the madman!'

Four strong men came to drag Michael away, but he cried, 'Wait! Which one of you is her brother? She gave me a token for you. Please, listen to me and do as I ask if you would save your sister's life. Please open the coffin and look inside.'

The brother took the ring and recognised it. 'It is my sister's ring! Listen to him, open the coffin and let us see what is within.'

In front of the shocked mourners, they removed the coffin lid. There, inside, they found nothing but an old broom. They knew then that what Michael said was true. He was no madman, but was in fact their daughter's saviour.

The girl's brother and her parents were grateful to him, and, being a respectable family, they wanted to reward him. The brother rode to Barefield with Michael to collect his sister. When they reached the house, the girl was sitting rosy-cheeked by the fire, enjoying the soup Michael's mother had made for her. The brother brought her home with him, and she lived to a great age.

From that day, Michael was known as Savoury Flanagan. The girl had called him her saviour, but the people made that into 'Savoury'.

THE KERN OF QUERRIN AND THE STOLEN BRIDE

There was a young man living around Querrin shore, a fine, strong fellow of independent means. He had his own house and land, so he was beholding to no one, and the people called him the Kern of Querrin.

The Kern was a fine hunter, and he loved to go out shooting wild fowl along the shore of an evening. As darkness fell he would make his way stealthily along the sandy shore to the far strand where the wild geese gathered.

It was November Eve, the night we know as Halloween, when he crouched hidden behind an old ruin, waiting for the geese to gather on the strand. His breath rose into the frosty air like a wraith as he blew on his freezing fingers in the stillness of the night. A sudden loud splash called his attention. Believing it to be the wild geese, he raised his gun, making ready to fire when they would be within his range.

Watching in silence he saw that these were not geese, but some strange company moving along the strand in the dark of night. The skin on the back of his neck crawled and he knew this was no company of fowlers, but something uncanny. As the weird company drew closer, the Kern could discern the figures of four strong men, carrying a bier on their shoulders. Upon the bier was a body draped in a white cloth. When the men laid down their burden to take a rest, the Kern fired his gun into the air. The strange company scattered, running off in all directions, abandoning their mysterious burden on the shore, the night air echoing with their frightened shrieks.

The Kern came out from his hiding place to investigate the body on the bier. Lifting a corner of the embroidered white cloth, he saw the face of a beautiful young woman, pale in the starlight of the cold November Eve. By the gentle movement of her chest, and the faint mist of her breath, he knew that she was not dead, but in a deep trance-like sleep. He stroked her forehead and softly guided her into a sitting position, whispering to her all the time, as if she were a wild creature he were gentling. She opened her eyes and looked wildly around at her unfamiliar surroundings. Finally she caught the gaze of the Kern, and her wildness faded, as if she knew she could trust him to lead her to safety. She allowed the Kern to lift her from the bier. She took the arm he offered her and walked slowly with him along the shore.

They walked in silence through the cold night, until they reached his house. He built up the fire to warm the young woman, and colour returned to her face, but still she spoke not one word. The Kern was full of questions. Who was she? How had she come to be on a bier on his lonely shore? All remained unanswered. He made her a broth of vegetables to build up her strength, but she would not eat it, nor take the tea he offered her.

The mysterious young woman remained in the Kern's house for twelve months, but in all that time she spoke not one word, and neither ate nor drank. When a year had passed, and November Eve came again, the Kern returned to the far strand, in the hope he might find some answers to his many questions. As he passed the old fort of Lisnafallainge, he heard faint sounds of singing and pipes playing. Stopping to listen behind a ruined wall, he overheard men's rough voices, talking and laughing.

'Where shall we go to find a bride tonight?' said the first.

Another voice answered, 'Wherever we go, I hope our luck will be better than last year!'

'Oh, we had a rich prize, brothers. The Lord O'Connor's daughter, no less! Ah, but we lost her to that fool, the Kern of Querrin, who broke our spell. For this last year he has her in his house, but little pleasure he's had of her!'

A fourth voice broke in, 'And so it will remain, for she will not eat nor drink nor speak until he serves her a meal on her own embroidered tablecloth.'

As he listened, the Kern remembered the embroidered white cloth that had covered the girl when she lay on the bier. What had he done with it? It was now the top cover on the young woman's bed. So was this her own tablecloth, and could it really break the spell?

He raced home and straight away burst into the young woman's bedroom, where he pulled the white cloth from her bed. 'Wake up! I know who you are, and how to break the spell! Come with me.'

Wrapping a warm blanket around her shoulders, the girl followed the Kern to the kitchen and watched as he laid the white cloth on the table. The Kern laid meat and drink, bread and cheese on the cloth, and bade her sit, eat, drink. She sat at the table and began to eat, small mouthfuls at first, then washed it down with water, wine. She smiled as the memory of tastes and flavours returned and her appetite was gradually restored. At last, when she had eaten and drank her full, words came to her. 'Thank you, good Kern of Querrin, for your kindness this past year, and for breaking the spell laid upon me. Now that speech is returned to me, I can tell you my story.'

'I am ready to hear it, good lady, and glad to have been of service. Now tell me please, what is your name?'

'My name is Maire, and I am the daughter of Lord O'Connor of Kerry. This day twelve months past, I was to be married to a young man. My father had arranged it all.

I did not know the young man, but had heard only good of him, and was happy enough to wed. The date was set, and when the guests were all assembled, a sudden sickness came upon me. I grew faint and fell into a swoon. I knew nothing more until you woke me on Querrin shore. That broke part of the spell upon me. The white embroidered tablecloth was a wedding gift from my father. Now you have served me a meal upon it, all that strange magic is dispelled, and I am free at last!'

The Kern of Querrin made his coach ready and returned Maire to her father's house. The Lord O'Connor of Kerry was only delighted to have his daughter alive and well. A great feast was held, and speeches made and stories shared.

The Lord O'Connor could see the Kern was a fine young man, of good character, wisdom and wit. He invited the Kern to stay a while, all the time wondering what he could do to repay him for his kindness and care of his beloved daughter. At length, he offered his daughter's hand in marriage, and the Kern, delighted, did not refuse. A wedding was arranged, and when the guests were all assembled, no spells befell the wedding party, unless they were spells of love. As far as I know, the feasting and the dancing went on all night long. They may be dancing yet. The young couple lived happily together and only good followed all the work of their hands from that day on.

References:
The Grateful Dead: SFS (1937-38) Mrs Brew, Tullycrine, Ennis told to Bridie Brew, Tullycrine NS, p.93.
Savoury Flanagan: SFS (1937-38) Thomas MacMahon, Spancilhill told to Ethel MacMahon, Spancilhill, Drumbanniff School, Crusheen, p.9.
The Kern of Querrin and the Stolen Bride: Lady Wilde, *Ancient Legends, Mystic Charms, and Superstitions of Ireland* (Ward & Downey; London, 1887).

8

SAINTS, SINNERS, MIRACLES & MARVELS

SIGNS OF THE SAINTS

At one time the whole of Ireland must have been half full of holy men and women. Throughout County Clare there are wells dedicated to these saints, and here and there they have left their mark on the landscape. In some places it is literally footprints, while in others it may be the imprint of their knees in prayer, an austere stone pillow, or a row of stones on a hillside where they have cursed thieves and turned them to stone.

Here's a wee story of three saints in search of a place to settle. It is just possible that they invented surfing, something that is very popular on Clare's beaches nowadays.

Maire loved the sea. She loved the sound of the soft waves, shushing onto the pebbles of the shore. She loved the breeze and the smells it carried to her. She loved the song of the birds as they wheeled above her or came to land, bobbing on the waves. She did not usually mind her mother sending her to gather seaweed from the shore at Ross. It gave her the freedom to cast off her stockings and shoes, put down her basket, and dance along the sand, for there was no one there to see her. So long as she returned with a full basket, no one would care that she danced with a heart free and light as a spirit of the waves, or sang with the birds on the rocks.

This day, as she was crossing the green field, she saw there were three holy brothers working on the shore. Maire knew them by the way they wore their hair and their long robes. While they were busy at their task, she took off her stockings and shoes and laid them on a rock. She lifted up the bottom of her skirts to keep them from getting wet. She moved along the line of the shore with the grace of a dancer. As she was skimming flat stones into the water and laughing as they bounced on the waves, one of the brothers turned to watch her, and he said, 'Hasn't that girl just got the loveliest little white feet?'

The other two men turned to look, then quickly turned back, telling the first brother that he had sinned. Firstly for watching the girl at all; then for noticing her bare feet; and worst of all, for passing a remark that drew their attention to the girl's bare feet and caused them to commit a sin too!

The holy brothers decided they must pit themselves against the elements in penance for their sins. It was the habit of holy men and women in those days to take themselves away from the temptations of the world and to live in caves or sleep in rocky beds on remote islands. It seemed that the shore of Ross was not remote enough to save them from temptations of the flesh.

Maire watched as the first brother sought out a large flat stone and, taking it to the water's edge, he stepped upon it.

Balancing on his flagstone on the waves, he raised his arms and said a prayer, trusting that the tide would carry him wherever God wished him to go. The other two brothers followed his example on flags of their own.

The three sailed down around Loop Head and into the mouth of the Shannon. The first came in to land at Kiltrelice, and where he stepped ashore a well sprung up. Today it is named after him, St Cuan. The second brother, St Creadaun, landed at Carrigaholt, and a well arose there; while the third brother, whose name was St Cronan, came ashore a few miles along at Kilcronan, where a well still bears his name.

∞

St Colmkille is famous for copying a book that caused a huge upset, led to a great battle and the saint being exiled from Ireland. Colmkille sailed across the sea to Iona, where he built his church and started converting the Scots. None of those things happened in County Clare. What he did here was leave the mark of his boot-nails on a rock.

On Mount Callan there was a place where people used to gather to celebrate the festival of Lughnasadh, marking the beginning of harvest time. Now I don't know whether it was that time of year, but anyway, St Colmkille was travelling from Galway to Mount Callan one time, and he had a dog with him for company. As they got near to Mount Callan, a hare leapt up out of the grass and the dog chased it, with the saint running for all he was worth to keep up at his heels. The saint and his hound chased the hare to Cluain Caolan, where it went out onto the peninsula. The hare took a great leap across the breadth of the lake, which was no mean feat as the lake was 300 yards wide at that point. The hound and the saint followed where the hare had leapt, and there are marks still on a large stone where they landed. Now I do not know if they caught the hare, but there are three sets of prints on that stone: the tracks of the hare, the dog's paws and the mark of the iron nails of St Colmkille's boots.

In the time of the saints, there were three holy men who lived together in a cave in the parish of Ballycorrick, just north of Clondegad Bridge. Their names were St Scriobhan, St Nuadan and St Ruadh. It seems that even the best of us cannot be at peace with our fellows at all times. One day, the three saints had a serious difference of opinion on some ecclesiastical matter. Although they could find no common ground on the matter, they could at least agree that they must go their separate ways. St Scriobhan would remain at Clondegad, as he had been there long before the others had settled. Scriobhan's spartan bed is still there in a narrow recess beneath an overhanging rock at the top of the waterfall in the Clondegad River. The other two would travel abroad in search of some new stretch of wilderness in which to speak to God. As the judgements of men had proved lacking, they let a higher power decide the matter of where they should go. The two each made a gad of rushes and threw them out into the river, planning to travel in whatever direction their gad took. Nuadan's gad went against the current, so he travelled up-river, and settled at the place now called Tubbernuadan, or Nuadan's Well. Ruadh's gad went with the river and he travelled southwards, settling near Ballynacally. Since then the parish has been called Clondegad, or the meadow of the two gads.

St Mochulla of Tulla kept a tame bull that he had trained to carry messages for him. At this time, the saint was busy building his church on the hill at Tulla. He was so engrossed in his work that he had no time to stop to get provisions or cook his dinner. So, he made an arrangement with the monks in Ennis. They would cook him some dinner when they were making their own, and St Mochulla's blessed bull would collect it. He would fasten a bag around the bull's shoulders and send it off to Ennis. The bull knew the way and would walk there and back quite happily, serving his master. There would, on occasion, be more than food in the bag the bull carried from Ennis to Tulla. Whatever the saint needed would be sent this way: perhaps holy books or relics, or maybe even gold.

A gang of seven thieves got to hear about the clever bull and planned to rob the beast. It was not so much the bull itself, as what he might be carrying that they were after. They knew the route the bull was used to travelling and hid themselves on Classagh Hill, ready to waylay him on his return from Ennis. As the bull approached, the thieves leapt upon him, beating him with sticks and emptying the bags. The bull gave one almighty roar, so loud that he could be heard in Tulla. St Mochulla laid down his tools when he heard the terrible call. 'Who dares to harm my good servant?' he cried. He prayed for the safety of the bull and cursed the men that dared to hurt him.

Right then the men on the distant hill froze as they were, suddenly turned to stone. Perhaps one or two of the robbers escaped the curse, for today there are only four stones standing in a row on the hill. The place is known as Knocknafearbreaga, which means the 'hill of the false men'.

ST SENAN

For all that Clare is a large and extensive county, it is the one county that St Patrick never set foot in. The closest he came was to near Foynes in County Limerick. Many people from West Clare, came to hear him speak, it being simple enough to cross the Shannon by boat. He spoke to them directly, telling them that a child born in Corca Bascin would do for Clare what he, Patrick, had done for the rest of Ireland.

At that time, in some places the older faith lived side by side with the new. Many druids recognised in the Christ that the saints spoke of, a master of the elements, a great druid.

On the hill of Ballyvaskin there are huge stone walls where the princes of Corca Bascin lived from before the birth of Christ until the Battle of Clontarf. Here lies the Grianan, a triangular section of ground that would have been a sheltered, sunny spot, where members of the court could take their ease. It was here that the chief held his annual feast and assembly for the people of West Clare. He did this once a year, and guests came from every part of West Clare, rich and poor among them. The prince sat in his grand chair, and his druid sat by his side, in a place of honour as his wise counsellor. The druid paid no heed to all the assembled people, until

a couple, obviously very poor, entered. The druid stood up, bowed and invited them to please take his chair. The prince was puzzled and asked why the pair had been chosen. The druid spoke loudly and clearly so the whole assembly could hear: 'In this woman's womb, there is a child who will bring the Christ's message to the people of Corca Bascin. He will do many miracles and baptise the people.' And the druid foretold the coming of St Senan.

The woman's name was Congella. She was walking through a wood when her birth pangs began. When she grasped a bare branch of a tree it burst into bloom at her touch. A flat stone still marks the spot where she gave birth to her son in Moylough, near Kilrush. Even as a very young child he showed some miraculous qualities. He spoke his first words early, and seeming older than his years, his mother called him Senan, meaning 'old'.

Senan's father had a farm about 3 or 4 miles from Kilrush. The land was separated from the mainland by Poulmacsherry Bay. He kept a herd of cattle there. One day, his father told Senan to drive the cattle to the farm alone, as he had no time to do it. Senan obeyed his father's command and drove the cattle. When he reached the shores of the Bay he did not know how he would drive the cattle across the water with no one there to help him. Senan went down to the water's edge and he stretched his hand over the water. At once the waters drew back, left and right, and a straight dry road appeared. Senan led the cattle along the dry road across the bay. When they had crossed over, he drew his hand over the waters again and they closed up, as if they had never parted. He said then that the waters of Poulmacsherry Bay would never be parted again. One time, Clare County Council planned to make an earthen bank across the mouth of the Bay. They started the work, but just before it was completed, the tide swept it all away. The people remembered St Senan's words, and they did not try that again.

One day, the young Senan was out walking with his mother, and after a while she became thirsty. There was no spring close by, so he bent down and plucked a rush from the ground. Where he pulled the rush a lake sprang up, and a well of good spring water. These became known as St Senan's Well and St Senan's Lake, and people say the lake water has a cure for any disease of horses and cattle, and is good for crops, as well as a remedy for toothache.

On another occasion, Senan and his mother approached a village where they had hoped to spend the night. The people made it clear they were not welcome. They spoke crudely and made foul remarks that insulted Congella. When the pair still did not turn away, the people pelted them with stones. Senan's mother was most perturbed, but then her son told her that God avenges all wrongs done to his servants. After that, a plague fell upon that village and all of its inhabitants and their cattle died. Not one survived and the village itself was later swallowed up by the sea. Some people say this might be the sunken town of Kilstapheen.

As a young man, Senan was obliged to fulfil the duties of an ordinary man of his tribe. He therefore had to take part in an expedition against his tribe's enemies. The men of Corca Bascin marched against the men of North Clare, and did battle at Corcomroe. Senan took no part in the fighting, but he witnessed his tribe's defeat, and when he was pursued by the enemy, he hid himself inside a stack of corn. As the soldiers approached, suddenly the stack of corn seemed surrounded by flames, although both Senan and the corn were quite unharmed. Believing they had witnessed a miracle, the enemy soldiers spared Senan's life and let him go.

As he was making his way back to West Clare, Senan got very hungry and had to beg for food. He came to the home of a petty chieftain and asked for a bit of bread there. The chieftain was not at home and the servants refused to give him anything. Turning away still hungry, Senan was angry and cursed the food on their chieftain's table. The chieftain retuned soon after, and observed that the men at his table seemed to be talking nonsense and behaving oddly. When he asked his servants had anything unusual happened in his absence, they told him the saint had come begging but they had turned him away. The chieftain sent a messenger with a spare horse to bring Senan back with him for dinner. When Senan said a blessing on the food and enjoyed his hearty meal, the chieftain's men returned to their normal selves.

ST SENAN AND INIS CATAIGH

Senan had already shown signs of greatness from childhood. The miracles that manifested around him marked him out as touched by the hand of God. He travelled around Ireland, firstly in training as a monk at Kilnamanagh in Ossary. He made a pilgrimage to Rome, returning via the shrine of St Martin of Tours in France. He became a bishop and built churches around Ireland, living a long life as a man of God before he returned to West Clare to found his monastery there. A vision brought him back to a small island in the Shannon estuary, Inis Cataigh, now called Scattery Island.

The place was named after the Catach, a ferocious sea serpent or peist that lived in the waters that surrounded the island. This peist had a formidable reputation. She would capsize boats and devour the hapless sailors. She was rumoured to be over 3 miles in length, and could sleep coiled around the island, with her tail in her mouth. No one would dare go near the island for fear of the Catach. Some said she was a dragon, others described her as having the appearance of an enormous eel with a line of sharp barbs along the length of her back and a mouth full of sharp teeth. Near Kilrush there is a Gleann na Peists, where the monster was said to have deposited stones brought from the island.

Senan had no doubt heard stories of the Catach since his childhood. Now he must do battle with the peist if he was to claim the island for his holy community. It was an angel that transported Senan to the island to face the beast, and the very spot where the angel put him down is known as Knockanangel Hill. Senan spread his arms wide in prayer and called to the Catach to show herself and be ready to meet the new master of Inis Cataigh.

The Catach rose to the saint's challenge, advancing towards him with red eyes flashing like flames, spitting venom and stretching her jaws wide. The serpent swerved aside and swallowed Naroch, Senan's smith. However, the saint was able, with some words of power, to rescue the smith from the monster's jaws. Naroch was understandably shaken, but quite unharmed and enormously grateful.

Senan faced the beast without fear. He held aloft his golden cross and spoke, commanding her to give up her claim to the island. His words held power, his faith was certain, his trust in his God unshakable. The Catach, seeing the superior power of the saint, recognised there was no choice and surrendered. St Senan bound the monster with chains and banished her to Doolough Lake to the south of Mount Callan, commanding her to do no harm there. Only when the weather is wild does the serpent stir in that dark lake, and the surface of its waters seems to boil like a great pot over a stove. The beast herself is seen there once every seven years.

Having won the island from the Catach, St Senan prepared to build his church there. But the Catach was not the only one to oppose him. MacTail, the ruler of Hy Fidhgial, was furious when he heard the saint had taken possession of the island without his consent. MacTail sent his druid to confront the saint. The druid commanded a mist to cover the island, but St Senan dispelled that swiftly with a prayer. The druid then called darkness to fall, and again the saint overcame the druid's magic. Whatever the druid commanded, the saint dispelled. At last the druid left, disheartened, landing with his followers on Dair Inis, the island of oaks, where a great wave drowned them all as they stood at a rock known afterwards as Carrig an Draoi, the druid's rock.

MacTail then came to speak to the saint himself. He brought two horses with him, and ordered the saint to see to their care. When the saint refused, MacTail shouted and swore at him, and the saint called back, the excitement causing the horses to become distressed. As they reared and whinnied, the ground beneath the two fine horses gave way and swallowed them up. (That spot is known as Fan na nEac.) This only further stoked MacTail's fury.

'What a pointless waste of fine horse flesh!' MacTail railed against the saint. 'You do not scare me with your magic tricks, holy man. I am not afraid of you or your God, any more than I fear a shorn sheep!' Those words came back to haunt the unfortunate chief, when some time after he was thrown from his chariot when his horses shied at the sight of a sheep.

There was no spring well on the island at that time, and the monks suffered greatly from the lack of good water. They had to fetch it in buckets from the mainland, both for themselves and for their cattle and sheep. At last they spoke to St Senan about their plight. The saint rooted up some earth with his staff, and where he had dug, a spring well bubbled up, of good clear water. The monks were grateful to be saved the work of carrying water; now they could devote more time to praying. St Senan stuck his staff into the loosened ground beside the spring, and it took root and grew into a hazel tree.

Which makes me wonder, did the hazelnuts fall into the well, and were they eaten by a salmon? For that is what happened at another well hundreds of miles away where the River Shannon began, ah but that is another story altogether and not a story I have heard told down at this end of the Shannon.

At last, St Senan could begin to build his church. He built the Church of the Angel beside the spot where the angel had deposited him on the island. There is a mound of earth beside it that bears the marks of the saint's elbows and knees, where he knelt in prayer before banishing the Catach.

No Women Welcome

Many came from all over Ireland to visit St Senan. Holy men from other centres of the Christian faith, including St Brendan of Birr and St Kieran of Clonmacnoise, came to ask St Senan's counsel on sacred matters, such was his reputation for wisdom. The island was known for its hospitality. All visitors were made welcome – that is, unless they were female! The saint had one simple rule: he would allow no woman to set foot on the island, no matter how holy she might be. There were female saints who would have liked to visit, for reasons many and varied.

A woman named Cannera came from a community of holy women at Cill na gCailleach in Querrin. She was very sick; in fact, she knew that she was dying. Despite her sickness, she had travelled in the hope of speaking with the saint. It was her dying wish. A messenger brought word to the saint, and he looked offshore to where St Cannera lay in her boat. Despite her obvious devotion, still he would make no exception to his rule: no women on the island. She pleaded and said, 'Women are just as welcome to enter the kingdom of heaven as are men.' At this, the saint relented, sending one of his brothers out in a boat to give the dying woman her last rites. However, he still would not permit her remains to be buried on the island, but rather allowed her to be buried at the low tide mark, where the waves roll over her grave to this day.

St Brigit herself would have come, but St Senan would not allow even her on the island.

There was a kinswoman of St Senan's living with the holy community on Inis Cealtra in Lough Derg. She made a new set of vestments for the saint, and wanted to present them to him in person. Now, maybe she needed to do a final fitting to make sure they were not too long for the saint, but whatever her reasons, St Senan would have none of it. He sent her a message saying, 'Put the vestments in a wooden box and set it in the river. Let the water carry it to me with God's grace.' She duly did as he asked, and the wooden box floated down the Shannon. The vestments landed safely at Scattery Island, and I can only hope they did indeed fit the saint properly!

ST SENAN AND THE CLOG AN OIR – THE GOLDEN BELL

One day, a dispute arose between St Senan and some of the other holy brothers who had come to visit him. It was a simple difference of opinion, but they found they could not settle the matter by themselves. They were setting off on a journey and they prayed for guidance, asking God to give a sign to show which of them was in the right. All the brothers prayed fervently, their eyes wide open to see if there was a sign yet. After a short while, along the way between Kildimo and Farrighy, the brothers saw a golden bell descend slowly from the heavens. The brothers watched as the bell came to land at St Senan's feet. That was sign enough for them and they gave up their dispute. None of the brothers doubted St Senan's wisdom after that sign, and accepted that he was always naturally in the right.

The bell had powers of its own, as a bell from heaven no doubt should. It had the power to expose liars and criminals.

Once a Galway man lost a large sum of money. He believed it had been stolen, so he sent his servant to borrow the golden bell from St Senan. He was desperate to discover the culprit and see him suitably punished. St Senan happily gave the bell and the servant set off for home. Now, it so happened that it was the servant himself that was the thief, and now he was afraid that the bell would uncover his deceit. The man went into quite a panic, wondering what he should do. He threw the bell into the river and continued on home. When he reached Galway, he told his master that the saint would not give him the bell. His master replied, 'I believe you are a liar and a thief! What do you think this is sitting on the table before me?'

There on the table sat the golden bell. The servant was shaking all over as he confessed his crime. He gave back all the money he had stolen and the golden bell made its own way back to Scattery Island. The bell was still in use for testing truth or guilt in the nineteenth century.

St Senan was buried on Scattery Island, and all the chieftains of west Clare were buried there too. An elder tree grew by his grave, and it was considered unlucky to cut or break a twig from it.

For all his misogyny, St Senan's protection over the island meant that in its later years, when the Shannon river pilots and their families lived in a street of houses there, no Scattery Island woman ever died in childbirth.

Perhaps, after his death, with the wisdom of hindsight, St Senan relaxed a little and extended his blessings to women after all!

THE OLD WOMAN AND THE PIG

There was an old woman who lived in County Clare long ago, who was the proud owner of a pig. The pig was her beloved prize possession and she cared greatly for it. So, when the pig suddenly fell sick one day, the old woman was terribly worried about it. The pig would eat nothing and simply lay on the floor groaning, while its breathing came in loud fits and starts.

There being no vet around the place in those days, the neighbours suggested the woman should go and visit the parish priest, to see if he could help. The power of prayer being a great thing, perhaps a cure might come from that.

The old woman went at once to see the parish priest and told him her sad story. The priest was doubtful that he could help, having no experience with animals himself, but the woman would neither be satisfied, nor silent, unless he would come to see the pig.

At last the priest relented and came to the old woman's house. He knocked upon the door and the woman brought him inside. There he found the sick pig, lying in the corner of the room. He leaned over the pig, and the smell was something terrible. He wanted to hold his nose and could hardly help but retch at the stench. Mostly he wanted to get out into the fresh air as quickly as possible, but for the old woman's sake he said a few quiet words over the creature as if he was in prayer.

'Well now, if you live, you'll live, and if you die you'll die. But whether you live or you die, you are no great loss.'

The old woman was grateful and thanked the priest for his 'blessing'.

As it happened, the pig recovered and was soon back on its feet. The woman was delighted and believed that the pig lived thanks to the priest's few quiet words.

Some months later the old woman heard that the priest himself had taken sick. In fact, the poor man was gravely ill. The doctors said that he would die, and the only thing that might save him was if he was able to give one long, hearty laugh.

When she heard how sick he was the woman decided she must visit the priest before he would meet his maker.

She knocked on the door, but the housekeeper would not let her in. She argued and made her case, and at last she was let in past the doctors and the relatives to the sick room where the priest lay dying. He was a sorry sight: his hair was matted, his skin was grey, and he looked frail and old despite his years as he lay propped up on a pile of pillows under a plump embroidered eiderdown.

Going over to his bedside she spoke the words which the priest had uttered over the sick pig, believing them to be a blessing with great healing power. 'Well now, if you live, you'll live, and if you die you'll die. But whether you live or you die, you are no great loss.'

When he heard these words, the priest burst into a hearty laugh. This being just what the doctor had ordered, he was immediately cured and soon back to his old self.

PRIDE

There was a good but ignorant man who never went to mass. In all the rest of his ways he lived well, never speaking a bad word about any of his neighbours and treating all he met with respect and politeness. He worked hard and stayed away from liquor.

But the people told the priest that he would not go to mass, and so the priest paid him a visit. Well, the good man had not heard about prayers and did not know that he should be going to mass at all! So when it came time for mass the next time, he went along.

When he sat down, there was a sunbeam in front of his seat. The good man took off his coat and hung it on the sunbeam and there it stayed, just as the good St Brigit had hung her cloak on a sunbeam to dry long ago!

The next time he went to mass, there was the sunbeam again. The man took off his coat to hang it up. But this time it would not stay. He said, 'That was my first sin. I was too proud that the people had noticed the small miracle.'

THE LITTLE ARK OF KILBAHA

There was a time in the 1850s when the practice of Roman Catholicism was suppressed on the Loop Head Peninsula. Protestant landlords would give the priests no land for the building of a church.

Marcus Keane, a land agent who lived in a large house in Kilbaha, was responsible for the building of a Protestant church there and a number of schools on the peninsula where the Protestant faith would be taught. As the people were only beginning to recover from the Great Famine, the food provided to children at these schools proved a huge incentive to families renouncing their Catholicism. Considerable pressure was also put on tenants who were threatened with eviction if they would not surrender their religion.

The parish priest, Fr Meehan, began building schools for the Roman Catholics in order to preserve his faith on the peninsula. He knew that what was needed was a church where his flock could gather, but there was no building available. He held mass in his own home for a while, but was soon evicted. He, along with other priests, tried a number of temporary solutions, including tent-like shelters of wooden poles and canvas, without success, as the wind and rain proved too strong for them and continually blew them down.

At last an inspired idea came to him. If there was no land in the area that was not owned by Protestant landlords, then he would use the strip between the sea and the shore, which was owned by no one. This space between the high and low tide lines was a kind of no man's land, and it would surely not be illegal to congregate there.

So far so good, but what would he do for a shelter? Well, around that same time, the bathing machine was in use on fashionable beaches. These 'machines' were small huts on wheels that were used to preserve everyone's decency. Bathers would change into their bathing costumes and be wheeled into the sea, where they could slip into the waters without their bodies being exposed. Did Fr Meehan find his inspiration from seeing these in use on the beach at Kilkee? Whether it was divine inspiration or a bit of lateral thinking, who knows. The priest had a carpenter in Carrigaholt build him a wooden shed on wheels, with windows on both sides and an altar opposite the door. When it was finished, he had it brought to Kilbaha where it was no doubt greeted warmly.

Each week he wheeled this strange contraption down to the space between the tide lines and held a mass on the shore in Kilbaha from the 'Little Ark' as it began to be called. His faithful congregation of up to 300 knelt in the mud and

sand to pray, regardless of the weather. There were marriages sealed there, and babies baptised in the odd little shelter between the sea and shore. People came from far and wide to see this strange phenomenon, and many were amazed at the lengths people would go to to practice their faith.

Some years later, land was finally granted to Fr Meehan for a church building at Moneen. Whilst the church was being constructed, mass was still celebrated from the Little Ark, which was transported to Moneen and eventually moved into the building. The Little Ark was moved into its final resting place within an annexe to the church building, where it remains to this day.

SAINTS ISLAND

At one time there used to be a lot of traffic on the River Shannon. It was almost easier to move about on the water than on the land, and the river would have been one of the main thoroughfares. There are a lot of islands in the Shannon, and one of them, near Bunratty, is called Saints Island.

There were people called McInerney who lived on that island. They kept a few cows; Mrs McInerney, she had a number of chickens; and her husband, he went out fishing in his boat. They had a baby, probably the first of many that would follow, God willing.

One day, when Mr McInerney was out fishing, away from the island, a boat came up the river and pulled in on the shore. Mrs McInerney didn't see it for she was in the back room at the time, settling the baby to sleep.

There was just the one man in the boat, a rough-looking fellow who was up to no good. He saw the house, the only house on the island, and he headed towards it. He was calling out 'Hello. Hello,' pretending to be friendly, but nobody came out to see who was approaching. Since it looked as if no one was around, he just went right inside the house and started opening the dresser drawers and pulling out whatever he found in there. He was looking for money and gold watches, jewellery, that kind of stuff. He didn't find any of that, nor anything else that was much use to him, so he went through to the other room then, to see could he find any valuables.

All this time Mrs McInerney was in the other room. She must have fallen asleep herself when she was settling the baby, until the sound of doors banging and drawers being opened and things being thrown about must have woken her up. She jumped up and was standing there frozen with fear, with the baby, her most precious possession, in her arms, when the robber came into the room. There was nowhere she could hide. The man had the wild look of a hunted animal in his eyes. There was a scar down the side of his face and his hair was all scraped over to one side.

When he saw her, he shouted at Mrs McInerney to give him her valuables. Mrs McInerney said, 'The only thing I have of any value is my own baby boy.'

'Well now Mrs,' said the robber, 'If there's nothing else worth anything, then I'll take the child. There's rich folk in London would pay good money for a healthy baby boy!' The robber threatened terrible things if she would not give him the child. Mrs McInerney backed away as he reached to grab the child from her arms. She got past him through into the other room, all the time crying out a desperate prayer to all the saints that she knew the names of to save her child. The first thing she saw in the other room was the milk churn. A sudden inspiration came to her: she could hit the man with the churn staff!

It must have taken all her courage and all her strength,

but when the man came after her, she hit him over the head. He fell down dead and Mrs McInerney and her child were saved, thanks to all those saints she had prayed to. After that the island was known as Saints Island.

MUIRISHEEN FODERA FOLLOWS HIS DREAM

There was a man called Muirisheen who lived in Fodera, down near Loop Head, in a mean little cabin with a door painted red, a briar bush by its side and a rough path leading down to the shore. He never had much at all, but he lived well enough and slept easy in his bed each night. Until one night Muirisheen had a strange dream that woke him early in the morning.

In the dream he was on the quays in Limerick where he met a man who gave him gold and treasure, so that he would never be in need again. The first night he dreamed it, he thought, 'Well, that would be a fine thing to meet on the quays in Limerick!' and he laughed at himself and fell back to sleep again.

The next night, when he woke from the same dream, he laughed again at his wishful thinking. But when he dreamed the same dream on a third night, he began to think there might be more to it. He went to see a little old woman who lived nearby and told her about the dream. She advised him, 'Well, unless you go to the quays in Limerick, you will never know what awaits you, whether it be good or bad. What will you do Muirisheen?'

Muirisheen decided to set off that morning, before he could change his mind, to see what fortune he might find on the quays of Limerick. It was a long way round to walk by land, so Muirisheen got himself a place on a boat bringing turf to the city. The boat stopped at Scattery Island and some of the other small places along the Shannon on the way.

When they reached the quays of Limerick, Muirisheen helped the men unload the cargo of turf. When that was done, he leapt ashore and walked up and down the busy quays. There was so much activity there, with men and ponies carrying loads from the boats into the town, he didn't know where to look for his fortune. He wandered up and down the quays, searching for the man and the gold. He asked a number of people, if they had his fortune, but no one had the slightest clue what he was talking about. At last he sat down on a big stone and took off his hat, wiped his brow and started to wonder if he was just a madman who had come to Limerick following a false and foolish dream. Had he made a wasted journey? Perhaps he should start walking for home? There was a long journey ahead of him if there was no boat going down the Shannon that day.

As he sat there, lost in his thoughts, a man in a black overcoat and a tall hat came up and asked Muirisheen what was the matter with him, 'Are you lost, man? Are you looking for someone? Can I help you find your way?'

'I am glad that you asked me, sir. Thank you for your kindness and may God reward you. My name is Muirisheen Fodera and I came all the way to Limerick quays to seek my fortune. You see, I have had a dream for three nights running that I would meet a man here who would give me gold and treasure. I have been here half the day now, and found no one, no gold, nothing. Am I just a fool to have come this way?'

'Hah!' said the man in the black overcoat, 'I have also dreamed of finding gold and treasure. These last three nights I dreamed I found gold under the threshold stone of a little mean cabin in a place called Fodera. I saw the place clearly in the dream. The door was painted red, there was a briar bush by the side, and a rough path leading to the shore. Sure, they are only dreams, man; there is no truth in them. I would not waste my time looking for such a place, when I know that if I work hard enough here in Limerick, I will make my own fortune. Go home, Muirisheen Fodera, go home.'

Muirisheen shook the man's hand, 'Thank you for your wise counsel, sir. May you never know how it has helped me. What a fool I was to seek my fortune here. I will leave for home at once.'

Muirisheen asked all along the quays until he found a boat heading down the Shannon that day.

When he reached his mean little cabin, he fetched the crowbar and set to work. After an hour or two he managed to raise up the threshold stone. Underneath there was a wooden chest with metal catches sitting upon an old griddle. Muirisheen raised the lid and found it full of gold coins and jewels. He sat himself down and wiped his brow, and laughed out loud, 'Ha ha, so is Muirisheen Fodera a fool to follow his dream? Well, if I am, then it is a rich fool I am!'

He kept the griddle, for there was decoration on it and something written, but Muirisheen could not read it. He polished it up and put it on his mantelpiece, and wondered what he would do with the gold.

A few years later a poor scholar travelling around the country stopped at Muirisheen's house for refreshments. It was no longer a mean little cabin, as Muirisheen had made a few improvements to the place. The scholar was enjoying his cup of tea from the china cup, when he saw the griddle above the mantlepiece. 'Where did you get that griddle?' asked the poor scholar.

Muirisheen was reluctant to answer. 'Why do you want to know?' he asked suspiciously.

'Well,' said the scholar, 'it is the words engraved upon it, my dear host, that may be helpful to you.'

'I kept it for the decoration on it. It looks fine there above the fireplace, does it not? I could not read the writing. Tell me, scholar, what does it say?'

'It says, 'Whatever is found on top, there is as much again beneath.' Does that have any meaning for you, sir?'

Muirisheen did not wait to answer. He went at once to fetch his crowbar and shovel. The poor scholar watched amazed as Muirisheen raised the threshold stone and dug down into the gravel beneath. The shovel rang out as it struck something. Muirisheen cleared away the gravel and brought up another chest. When he raised the lid, there was another heap of gold coins and jewels!

The poor scholar helped carry in the chest, and Muirisheen rewarded him with a pocketful of gold.

TREASURE AND TREACHERY

There was a story recorded up around Caherhurley about one of the last of the O'Briens. This man was returning over the mountain to Kincora, on his way home from a battle. He was not travelling alone, but had with him a faithful servant who had been with him for many years. When they reached the point where Kincora came into view, instead of the fine palace in all its glory, they saw it masked by smoke and flames leaping all around it. O'Brien feared that his end was surely near. He knew he dared not go to Kincora himself, as his enemies were awaiting his return. Instead, he told his good servant to go to Kincora in stealth, trusting that the enemy would not harm him. He instructed the servant to search in a particular location and to bring his treasures from their hiding place to O'Brien, up on the mountain.

As evening drew near the servant obediently set off and quickly reached the spot his master had described. He found O'Brien's treasure, filled a sack with gold coins and glittering jewels, and made his way back to the mountain under the starlit sky. O'Brien and the servant worked together to conceal the treasure securely under a pile of stones. When this was done, greed overcame the servant. Only he and O'Brien knew the whereabouts of the treasure, and the two of them were alone on a lonely hillside. No one need ever know. The servant took up a rock and struck his master. O'Brien fell down dead, and the servant covered his body with stones. Now no one but him knew the location of O'Brien's treasure.

The servant let it lie well alone for a few years. Indeed, he thought little of the treasure on the mountain, until the time came that he was to be married. Then he confided in his wife-to-be that he knew the location of a hidden treasure, and that he had best go and ensure it was still safe up on the mountain. Of course he did not tell her how this treasure had come into his possession.

It was a muggy sort of a day when he took himself up the mountain again. The air was warm and heavy, as if thunder might come. When he came to the place where the gold and jewels were concealed, he went first to stand over the grave of his former master. Perhaps he meant to say a prayer, or to ask forgiveness, but that we will never know, for before he opened his mouth to say a single word, he was struck by lightning. As the thunder clouds rolled over, he fell to the ground, stone dead beside the grave of the man he had slain for greed.

When he did not return home as expected, the bride gathered a party of men to search for him. They were not long up on the mountain before they found the servant's body, and close by, another corpse. Now the story became clear, and the servant's treachery was discovered.

The men buried the two bodies there on the mountain. They buried O'Brien's remains in a spot where the sun could always shine on his grave. The faithless servant's body they buried in a spot where the sun never reaches. There were no grave markers erected, so today no one knows quite where on the mountain those graves are to be found. Nor do we know if the treasure was ever discovered. For all I know, it may be lying there still, under its covering of stones, just waiting for some fortunate walker on the East Clare Way to find it.

References:
Saints: SFS (1937-38), Wan O'Dwyer and May Keane heard this from their parents, reel 180; SFS (1937-38) Thomas Casey and M. McDonnell, Lough Burke, Kilmaley, told to John Casey, Feighro, Kilmaley, p.54; SFS (1937-38), Tim Sexton, Deermade, told to John MacGrath, Lissycasey, p.450, Reel 177.
St Senan: SFS (1937-38) Paddy Malone heard from Martin Howard, Ballyvaskin, reel 179; Patrick Cleary and others, recorded by Michael Twomey, Burrane School, reel 176; p. 19, reel 179; John Cunningham, reel 180; Anon, Kilrush, reel 181; *Folklore of Clare*, T.J. Westropp (Clasp Press; Ennis, 2000).
The Old Woman and the Pig: SFS (1937-38) Kitty Williams Carnacalla, Kilrush told by her mother, reel 180.
Pride: SFS (1937-38) Joseph Bonfield, reel 180.
Saints Island: SFS (1937-38) Mrs J. Quinn, Cloughlea, Sixmilebridge, Sixmilebridge NS, p.387.
Muirisheen Fodera Follows His Dream: SFS, Batt Scanlon, Doonaha.
Treasure and Treachery: SFS (1937-38) John Malone, Caherhurley, Caherhurley School, p. 279, reel 174.

9

LAKES, WAVES & SUNKEN LANDS

ECHOES OF ATLANTIS: THE THREE CHIEFS AND THEIR SISTER

There were three chiefs who lived long ago near Kilbaha and they had one sister. The three chiefs each built themselves a castle. The first made his castle at Dun Dallon; the second near Cross, and the third in Carrigaholt. The sister lived with the second chief at his castle in Cross. Not far from this castle, out in the Shannon, there was an island and on it was a beautiful village called Kilsteefeen.

Across the Shannon in Kerry there was a man who had some power of magic. This magician had seen the sister from the top of his high tower and taken quite a fancy to her, and he wanted to bring her to live with him in Kerry. Her brothers were ready to fight to protect her as a prophecy stated that if their sister were to marry, then a great disaster would befall them.

In those times cattle raiding was a common pastime among the tribes. They were all at it, and when one crowd stole away your cattle, there was nothing for it but to go out on an adventure and steal them back, and bring some of their cattle back along with your own. It was great sport altogether!

One day there came a party of thieves, intent on driving away the brothers' cattle. The three brothers rode out after them, and they left a druid to guard their sister, who was almost as precious to them as their cattle.

The druid worked his protective magic around the sister and the castle where she lived. He chanted and he prayed. He lit a candle and meant to keep it burning while the brothers were away.

Now, the Kerry magician had a few tricks of his own! He had a magical ring that could change colour and tell him about the state of things in the country. He knew by the colour of his ring that the girl's brothers were away from home. He sent a serpent that circled around, whispering and hissing, and caused the druid to fall asleep. Without his watchful eye, the candle flame faltered and went out. Seeing that the coast was now clear, the Kerry magician got into his boat and made his way over the water to steal away the girl.

The druid woke up with a sudden start, surrounded by darkness. He saw that his protective flame had died. He knew it was the Kerry man's magic at work, and that he would be already on his way across the water. The druid was furious to have his spell of protection broken. He called on the elements: earth, water, air and fire. He called the powers of the wind and waves to rise up and drown the boat and all within it.

The wind blew strong across the Shannon, growing in strength and fury. The waters answered its call, rising higher and wilder, foaming and spitting as they engulfed the magician's boat. The Kerry magician uttered curses as his boat was swallowed by the waves. He cursed the wind and the waters. The waves continued to grow fierce and high, until they advanced like a great wall of water towards the shore of the beautiful island of Kilsteefeen. The houses and spires, the cattle and all the people on the island vanished beneath the fury of the waves.

It is said that once every seven years the island rises from the Shannon, and is seen for a day. I would not want to be the one who sees it, for it is unlikely that good fortune is in it.

THE SUNKEN CITY OF KILSTUIFFEEN

Where the waters of Liscannor Bay lie today, there was once a beautiful city called Kilstuiffeen. Fishermen have been known to catch the scent of its flowery meadows, or to hear the ringing of bells from its church towers as they sail across the bay, and have lived unharmed to tell the tale. People say it would be a different matter if they caught a glimpse of its shining towers and spires beneath the waves. Anyone who sees the sunken city is doomed to meet their death within the year.

Ruaidhin, Ceannir and Stuiffeen were three bold warrior brothers who lived in the west of county Clare long ago, before the days of the saints. Each brother had his own lands and castle: Ruaidhin's stronghold was at Moher-Ui-Ruaidhin near Hag's Head and the Cliffs of Moher; Ceannir's fort was at Liscannor, and Stuiffeen's was the famous palace of Kilstuiffeen that once stood where a rocky reef now lies out in the bay between Liscannor and Lahinch.

All three brothers had extraordinary powers, but Stuiffeen had a particular gift. He could draw a veil of invisibility over his golden city at will. If he needed to leave his palace, he could summon up the illusion of deep water and waves to cover it by speaking some words of power. He had a golden key to lock the palace gate behind him and secure his spell in place. Anyone who sought Kilstuiffeen would see only the sea, calm or stormy according to the weather of the day. As the illusion was for their protection, it did not affect those who lived there. Life went on as normal for Kilstuiffeen's inhabitants underneath the waves.

Being young, strong and hungry for adventure, the three bold brothers rode out one day in search of some sport. They rode as far as the southernmost point of Loop Head, where they found a number of stout long-haired cattle grazing on the grassy shore. The brothers rounded up the cattle and stole them away. The journey back was taking considerably longer as they drove the cattle, who continually wanted to stop and graze on the fine green grass.

Meanwhile, down at Loop Head, there were another three brothers who kept a herd of stout long-haired cattle. When the youngest was sent out early one morning to see if the cattle got water enough, he found a good number of the herd was missing. He saw the grass all ploughed up by horses' hooves and went running back to tell his brothers. 'Cattle raiders! They have taken half of our herd, and they are heading north!' Cattle rustling was the major sport for young men at that time. Quickly, the brothers secured their remaining cattle within an old lios or ringfort. They armed themselves with slings and swords and set off on swift horses, hoping to catch up with the raiders before they could reach the security of their own territory.

The Loop Head brothers rode like the wind. At last they spied Ruaidhin, Ceannir and Stuiffeen, along with the stolen cattle, in an old fort just past Miltown Malbay.

'Thieves! Blackguards! Did you think you could steal our cattle in the night and get away with it?' they yelled.

The raiders answered fiercely. First they threw insults at each other, and then they threw stones. Finally swords were drawn, and a bloody battle ensued.

The fighting went on until Ruaidhin, Ceannir and Stuiffeen lay dead on the ground. The brothers from Loop Head rode on to attack the strongholds of Ruaidhin and Ceannir, and to seize what plunder they could find in recompense for their troubles. They gathered up their cattle and drove them home. They would have raided Kilstuiffeen also, had its master not secured the gates with his golden key, rendering the palace invisible under the waves.

The golden key was lost that day. Some say it lies under the grave of Conan Maol on Mount Callan, but no key was found there when the grave was opened. Others say it was lost on the road to Liscannor, and that on the day it is found there Lahinch will be drowned. Others say an angry woman threw it into a lake on Mount Callan, where a monster swallowed it.

As the key has not yet been rediscovered, so Kilstuiffeen remains concealed today in Liscannor Bay, and its good people continue to live out their lives beneath the sea. They go about their business just as other folks do. Nothing from the world above disturbs them, except perhaps when a fisherman sends down his hook and line and accidentally catches up their dinner.

One day, two brothers named St Ledger went out from Liscannor in their boat fishing. They were having no luck; nothing was biting, so they rowed out further into the bay.

At last they felt a strong pull on their line, and began to haul it in. What they had caught was a big side of bacon and three potatoes, tied up in a linen cloth with a hand-written message attached. The message said, 'Clear for the shore. We are coming up!'

The men rowed as fast as they could, and just as they drew the boat up onto the shore, the tide suddenly went out. When they looked behind them, they saw Kilstuiffeen. They saw the golden roof of the palace, and the tall towers, and the ordinary houses of the people. They saw cattle grazing, and men going about their work and women spinning.

The brothers planted the potatoes they had brought up from beneath the waves and they got enormous yields from them. Those spuds spread all over the district and were known as 'Sallingers', after the men who found them.

THE FAIRY MAID OF INCHIQUIN LAKE

Inchiquin Lake, near Corofin, is one of the largest lakes in County Clare, but it may not always have been a lake.

There was once a castle belonging to Lord Inchiquin that stood right where the lake now sits. Not too far from the castle there was a well which provided good clear waters for the household. Every morning Lord Inchiquin would go to the well to drink. One morning, when he went for water, he saw a beautiful woman standing near the well. He fell in love with her and asked her to marry him. She told him she couldn't because she was not of his world, but was a fairy. He was very sad to hear this, and went home with a heavy heart. He sat all day thinking about her.

Next day he went to the well and the same fairy woman was there. He asked her again to marry him and this time she consented. After a few days they were married. They had two children, a girl and a boy. The father was very fond of his wife and two children, but he was also very fond of hunting. One day, when he was going hunting, his wife told him to come back alone if he loved her. He came back alone to please her. Next day she told him the same thing but this time he was frightened and brought back some of his huntsmen with him. When his wife saw that he did not come back alone, she thought he did not love her. She was very angry and, taking her two children, she returned to her own world. Before she left, she cast a spell over the well so that the water in it began to rise up. Soon it had reached the top of the well, then it overtopped it and began flowing out across the land. The water continued to flow from the well until it covered the castle and the land around it. It is said that the top of the castle can be seen on a calm day. From then on the lake was called Lake Inchiquin after the Lord Inchiquin.

NEVER DISTURB A WOMAN KNITTING

There is another tale concerning the formation of Lake Inchiquin. Before there was a lake or a castle or anything else there, a hurling field stood on the site of Lake Inchiquin. Boys used to come from all around the area to play hurling matches there. One day, there was a big crowd of lads playing hurling. The match was passionately contested and soon they began to quarrel when one of them had hit another. One said the other tripped him up on purpose; the other denied it. Voices were raised and fists were out, as the quarrel got louder and louder.

There was an old woman who lived in a cave on the side of Clifden Hill. She was sitting there, working at her

knitting and minding her own business, when the sound
of the boys' fighting caught her attention. She got up from
her rocking chair and, with her knitting under her arm, she
went marching down to see what was the cause of all the
noise. Finding the boys still fighting with each other, she
shouted at them crossly to stop it at once.

When the boys paid her no heed and just kept on with
their sport, the old woman took out one of her knitting
needles and stuck it deep into the ground. When she pulled
the needle out again, up sprang a well full of water. It spouted
up into the air, and ran bubbling over the ground, rising
higher and spreading further until it covered the whole field.

That was how Inchiquin Lake was made.

THE TOWN BENEATH THE LAKE

There was a woman who was on her way to Limerick, carrying big baskets of eggs and butter and a number of chickens to sell at the market. She was walking along by Cullaun Lake, when a big, wide road opened up in the middle of the lake. The water just rolled away to the two sides, like Moses parting the Red Sea! The woman saw a good surfaced road, and she thought it would shave some time off her journey if she took the road across the lake, rather than walking around it. She was crossing the lake when a strange woman appeared before her and asked, 'Where are you going?'

She told her, 'I am on my way to the market in Limerick to sell my eggs, butter and chickens.'

The strange woman said, 'Come along with me. I'll take you where you'll get a good price for your goods.'

The woman led her to a town under the water. The streets were wide and the houses tall and broad, and brightly coloured. There was a market square at the centre of the town where she soon sold her eggs, butter and chickens, and got gold sovereigns in return.

The strange woman appeared at her side again saying, 'It is late now. You would be best to stop here for the night.' She held out a hand to lead her to the steps of a grand house with pillars at the door.

The woman agreed she would walk no further that night, and consented to stay. The people there entertained her that night with stories, music and dancing, and they gave her the finest of food to eat. She slept that night in a four-poster bed in that grand house under the water.

When the morning came, I do not know what became of her, for she was never seen or heard of again in the area.

It may be that she is still living happily in that lovely town under Cullaun Lake.

THE LAKE OF THE RED EYE

Way back in the good old days, poets, storytellers and bards were admired and feared by the chiefs and masters. Bards enjoyed the patronage of kings. They could stay in the palace and they'd be well looked after for as long as they were there. They might dine at the king's table; be provided with the finest clothes; and enjoy privileges and perks granted to few others. All they had to do was tell stories and poems that made their patrons sound good and powerful. If a bard made a satire mocking his patron, however, the chief or king's reputation could be ruined. As a result, the bards might have been the most influential people in the country, a bit like the media today, and how they 'spin' a story influences people's opinions. Of course, the bards spent many years learning the stories that explained how the world had come to be the way it was, how places had got their names, and how to make poems that praised the worthy and satires that ridiculed the unworthy.

One time, King Connor Mac Nessa had a poet in his court in Ulster who went by the name of Aithirné the Importunate. Aithirne used to ask for all manner of difficult things, which Connor Mac Nessa was obliged to provide.

It was a quiet time in Ulster, with nothing much in the way of battles to be recorded in praise poems, so King Connor sent his talented yet scornful poet throughout the land of Ireland to sing praises to the other kings and princes in return for which, honour demanded, the poet could ask for whatever he wanted. If a prince refused even his most insolent demand it would give good reason for a battle.

Aithirné travelled throughout the country and came at last to the place where the provinces of Connacht and Munster met, near what is now called Mountshannon. Eochaidh Mac Luachta, King of Mid-Erinn, had a stronghold there overlooking the Shannon. Aithirné presented himself at Eochaidh's gates. 'I am come to sing praises to Eochaidh, lord of this place. Will you let me in to entertain you?'

The gates opened and the poet was led before the king. Servants brought water for him to bathe, and fine silks to dress himself after his long journey. A feast was prepared for him and he was made most welcome. Eochaidh called a gathering and all the people from miles around came to hear the Ulster bard proclaim. Aithirné created wonderful poetry for Eochaidh, praising his generosity and his hospitality, and then demanded his price.

'You are bound by obligation to pay me whatever I ask. Do you swear to keep this agreement, King Eochaidh?'

'I understand my obligation. Name your price and I swear I will meet it,' said the king.

'Then I demand, Eochaidh, in payment for my praises, an eye from out your head.'

The assembled crowd gasped in shock when they heard this unreasonable demand. After all, Eochaidh had only one eye as it was, his other being lost in a battle. The king, not wishing to call a war upon his people, nor be seen as ungracious nor inhospitable, obliged. With his own hand he plucked out his one remaining eye and handed it, dripping with blood, to the greedy and prideful poet. 'I honour my debts, bard. Remember that when you sing of me.'

Now that Eochaidh was blind, his good servant led him to the water's edge so he could bathe the wound. Kneeling down on the lough shore, he wrung out the cloth he had used to wash away the gore.

'Oh master!' cried the distressed servant. 'The water is all red with your blood!'

'Then let this lake bear that as its name, in memory of this day and this deed. Let it now be known as "Lough Derg Dheirc", the Lake of the Red Eye, from this day to the day the Shannon no longer runs to the sea.'

So, as the Shannon continues to flow to the sea, the lake is still known today as Lough Derg.

References:

The Three Chiefs and their Sister: SFS (1937-38) Arthur McGuire, Cross, told to Patrick McGuire, Kilkee, Boys School Kilkee, p.205.

The Sunken City of Kilstuiffeen: John O'Donovan & Eugene Curry, *The Antiquities of County Clare* (Clasp Press; Ennis, 2003), p.95; SFS, Aine ni Caisey, Lahinch; Thomas O'Brien, Lahinch; Brigid Collins from John Murphy, Glann, Enistymon.

The Fairy Maid of Inchiquin Lake: SFS (1937-38) Michael O Kennedy, Frances St Ennis, Scoil na m Brathar, Ennis, p.155.

Never Disturb a Woman at her Knitting: SFS (1937-38) Mary Kenny, Bankyle, Corofin, reel 178. (I just loved this because I love knitting!)

The Lake of the Red Eye: adapted from Patrick Kennedy's 'The Progress of the Wicked Bard' in *Legendary Fictions of the Irish Celts* (Macmillan and Company, 1891).

10

CREATURES GREAT & SMALL

There are many stories about white horses that come in from the sea. Hardly surprising, I suppose, when the western ocean is the land of Mananan Mac Lir, famous for his white horses, which can be seen galloping at the height of the waves in stormy weather.

Although many of these stories start off in the same way, with a farmer's crops being mysteriously eaten in the night, they lead us in some surprisingly different directions.

WHITE HORSES BY THE SHANNON SHORE

There was a farmer who used to grow a garden of oats for his own use in a field near the Shannon. There was no trouble at first, but as time went on he began to notice that in the morning his oats were all trampled and some had been eaten.

He decided to stay up all night to see who or what was destroying his field of oats. A neighbour agreed to spend the night out with him, in case he needed the help. They wrapped themselves up warm and settled down for the night at the edge of the field.

Just after midnight they noticed the first sounds approaching the oat field. They heard splashing and then hooves beating on the sand, and whinnying. Then they saw three white horses and a pure white foal come in from the strand, as if they had come out of the waves of the sea. The four horses began to feast on the field of oats.

The farmer knew that if you throw a clod of earth at a magical creature then it will do your bidding, so he scooped up a handful of earth from the edge of the oat field and threw the clod at the white foal. At once the foal stood as if frozen in place. The farmer went up to it and fashioned a quick makeshift bridle of string around its head and led it home.

He trained the horse to work for him and all was well. The horse grew and gave him a white foal each year for seven years. These fine foals brought him a good price.

When seven years had passed, he was out working near the shore when he heard the sound of a horse. He looked out over the Shannon waters but saw nothing. His horse,

who was tackled for ploughing, neighed loudly and then bucked and kicked, shaking herself free of her tackling. Helpless to stop her, his white horse ran for the Shannon waters. As she reached the edge of the shore, seven more white horses joined her and ran for the water. There was no way to stop them. All the horses splashed out into the river and disappeared under the water and were never seen again. Some people say that every white horse in County Clare is descended from that white horse.

THE SEA HORSE

There was a farmer living near Spanish Point, who sowed a field of corn, but every morning some of his corn was eaten. One night he stayed to find out what creature was eating his corn and he saw a white mare and a foal coming in from the sea. He tried to catch them but they were too fast for him. The next night he gathered a crowd of people. When the mare and foal came again, the crowd tried to catch them. They caught the foal, but the mare was too fast and wily for them and got away.

The farmer sold the foal to a rich man named Stackpoole. He trained it and the horse from the sea became one of the swiftest horses in the area.

Now, there were two brothers from the Fitzgerald family who lived near Stackpoole. One of the Fitzgerald brothers was called Vreasy and the other was Edmond. Vreasy Fitzgerald was a trained soldier and Edmond Fitzgerald was an ordinary man.

Edmond was up in Dublin, and one night he got invited to a grand ball. It was a smart affair, with the ladies and gentlemen in all their finest. Edmond danced a few

rounds with a lovely girl at the ball and went out walking
with her a few times after. Edmond was certain he was
in love with the girl. The only trouble was, there was an
Englishman who fell in love with the same girl. The two
men argued over who had the bigger claim to the girl. Of
course, in those olden times the men didn't understand
the nature of relationships like we do now. So instead of
talking to the girl about which beau she would prefer,
the two men argued amongst themselves. They were still
arguing about who had met the girl first or which of them
could provide the most comfortable living for her, when
the Englishman slapped Fitzgerald's face with his glove. If
actions speak louder than words, then that was a genteel
way of saying what children do in the playground when
they say, 'You're claimed!' It was a challenge to fight a
duel, with pistols.

Edmond Fitzgerald, being an ordinary man, was untrained in the use of firearms. He knew absolutely nothing about shooting, so he sent to Clare for his brother Vreasy, the soldier, to come and help him. There was no trains, buses or cars at that time; travel was by horses, which was not always as fast as you'd like it to be.

Vreasy asked Stackpoole if he'd lend him the sea horse so that he'd get up to Dublin in time to save his brother's life. Stackpoole gave him the horse, and ordered him to give the horse a half pint of white wine in Ennis and a pint of white wine in Limerick and then give it a loose rein to Dublin.

Vreasy Fitzgerald followed Stackpoole's instructions and it took him just four hours to reach Dublin, the sea horse ran so swiftly. But even for the sea horse, Dublin was a long way, and by the time they got to there the horse was covered in sweat. Vreasy got a vet to see to the horse, and then went on to the duelling place.

The Englishman arrived there with his witnesses, but when he saw no sign of Edmond, he said, 'Edmond Fitzgerald is a coward. He has not the courage to face me.'

Vreasy looked challengingly into the other man's eyes. 'You are mistaken, Englishman. I am Vreasy Fitzgerald, and I am here to take my brother's place in this duel.'

Vreasy removed his topcoat. The Englishman, who had been sure that he would win the duel, was disappointed to see that he was a military man. They tossed to see who would have the first shot, and the Englishman won. He fired his pistol, but the shot did no harm. When it was Vreasy's turn, he fired his gun and the Englishman fell down.

All that time the duel was going on, the vet was looking after the poor exhausted horse. He put the horse's feet into four firkins of butter, and that rescued the poor creature's feet. But for the butter, the sea horse might never have been able to run again. The horse slowly recovered its strength, but the journey to Dublin had left its mark on creature, for the horse had changed colour, from white to grey. When Vreasy brought the creature back to his owner, Stackpoole did not recognise him.

Vreasy entertained Stackpoole with the whole story of his ride to Dublin and the duel he had fought. Stackpoole found the story so enthralling that he said Vreasy could keep the horse as a reward for his victory.

There are farmers in Clare, especially in the west, who still boast that their horse was descended from the sea horse.

MacNamara's Foal

A few miles from Cullaun Lake, there are said to be two sets of hoof prints on a stone at Ballyhounan Farm. The people say that a horse and foal took one great leap from the Fergus Waters, 2 miles away, to that stone, and from there, in one further leap, they jumped another 2 miles to Cullaun Lake, where they disappeared again.

This horse and foal make an appearance in many stories from the area. Here they feature in a story of the MacNamaras.

The MacNamaras were a noble family in east Clare, and the remains of their castles and towers can still be found all over the locality. One of the MacNamara chieftains was famous as a great horseman. He lived in a castle close to Cullaun Lake, near Kilkishen.

Near the castle there was a meadow, but every morning the grass looked as if it had been grazed in the night. The chieftain gave his men instructions to keep watch that night. They were amazed by what they saw. A pure white mare and foal rose out of the waters and grazed for a while in the chieftain's meadow. When they'd had their fill, they returned to the lake and disappeared beneath the water. When they told the chieftain what they had witnessed, he ordered them to catch the horses, believing that they would add to his fame and power.

The next evening, MacNamara's men waited for the mare and foal to reappear. They circled around the horses as they were grazing, and tried to catch them with ropes. They managed to catch the foal, but the mare was too smart. She reared angrily and kicked out at them, managed to escape and leapt into the lake, vanishing beneath the water.

MacNamara was disappointed to lose the mare, but he knew the foal would be an exceptional horse. He trained the foal himself, and it was a quick and eager learner. It was not long before it was the finest war steed in the whole country. It was swift and sleek and courageous, and the chieftain and his horse won fame in many battle. The chieftain was proud of his achievement and considered the creature his prize possession, worth more to him than gold or property.

A few years passed by, and then one fine day the chieftain was enjoying his leisure, riding his proud steed along the shore of Cullaun Lake. Suddenly, the noon-day sky darkened, a wind arose from nowhere, and the white mare's head appeared above the water. She threw back her head, shaking her mane wildly behind her, and whinnied loudly. The steed threw back its head to answer her call with a whinny of his own. The steed reared and kicked, responding to his mother's irresistible call. Everything happened so fast, that MacNamara had no time to dismount. His horse galloped to the water's edge and leapt into the lake with the chieftain on its back. Horse and rider disappeared together beneath the waves, leaving nothing behind but the mark of the horse's four shoes on the rocks by the shore.

In the locality they say that MacNamara can be seen riding on his white horse around the lake once in every seven years, but that whoever sees him will not live out the year.

THE THREE COWS COME TO IRELAND

A long time ago there were no cows at all in the whole of Ireland. No doubt you will find that hard to believe, now that there are cows in all the fields wherever you look, but that is how it was in that old time. The people were hungry, and they desperately prayed that they would somehow get some food.

Then one day a mermaid came ashore from the sea and she lay there on the shingle until some of the king's men came down and carried her up to the palace. All the people adored her, she was so beautiful and gentle, and not quite like anyone they had seen before. She was clever too, and soon learned the language of the people. Then she said to them, 'I have been sent to you to tell you that a day will come soon when the cows will come to Ireland. Three cows will come: the black cow, the white cow and the red cow. They will fill the whole of Ireland with fertile and generous cattle, and their milk will flow freely to feed you all.'

The people were glad to hear it, for it meant they would get milk at last. They carried the mermaid about on a platform from house to house so that she could spread the good news of the cows coming soon. Wherever she went the people were happy to see her and there were great celebrations. They treated her like a queen and made a crown of flowers for her. The mermaid was wise and kind, and everyone loved her.

One day, the mermaid said, 'I am weary of living on the land. It is time for me to return to my own home and people in the sea.'

On May Eve the people gathered and carried her down to the shore so she could swim back to her own companions. Before she dived into the waves, she told all the people, 'On this day twelve months, you must come down to the shore, and there you will see the cows.'

The days passed by, and there was no sign of the mermaid in all that time. When a year had passed, the people gathered on the shore. All along the sands and the shingle, on the rocks and up on the high cliffs, crowded the people, old and young, watching for the cows. They were waiting from the moment the first light of the sun rose into the morning sky. When the sun was at its height, they heard a hushing, rustling sound and a big wave rose and spilled itself onto the shore, carrying with it the three cows. The people

stared. There stood Bo Finn, the white cow; Bo Dubh, the black cow; and Bo Derg, the red cow. All three were sleek and beautiful, with soft, dark eyes and long curved horns, white as the crescent moon. The people cheered to see them there, and the cows answered with gentle lowing.

The three cows looked around them and each set out, heading in different directions across the country. The black cow went to the south; the red cow to the north. The white cow went to the very centre of the country, and wherever she walked, the place was named after her.

From those three cows, all the cows in Ireland are descended.

A PLENTIFUL COW

During the famine times, things were very bad down in west Clare. Crops had failed, milk was scarce, and people were going hungry more often than not.

Mary and Pat lived in a tiny cabin in the district of Querrin with their three small children. They hadn't much, just what they stood up in, and their own good selves, but they did the best they could with what they had. One morning, however, Mary looked in the meal chest and was dismayed to see that there were only a few grains left at the bottom of it. What was she going to do to feed her husband and children? She had stretched their meagre supplies as far as she could, but now there was nothing left to stretch. Mary knelt down on the earthen floor and prayed harder than she'd ever done before, asking God to send something that would help them in their hour of desperate need. She'd grown used to her prayers going unanswered, but still she asked, hoping that this time sweet holy Mary and Jesus would hear her.

Later that same day a cow suddenly appeared outside the cabin door. It was a bonny grey cow, plump and sweet and seemed well looked after. Mary wondered where it had come from, thinking it must have strayed from some rich landlord's field.

The next day the cow appeared again. Mary could see that its udders were full of milk, but she didn't dare milk it. After all, she knew what would happen if she was caught milking the landlord's cow. Her neighbours obviously thought the same thing, as, although the cow wandered through the whole district of Querrin, no one dared to milk her.

On the third day, the cow came back to Mary's door. This time her udders were so full of milk the cow was lowing and pleading for Mary to milk her. Mary had the welfare of the poor cow at heart as sat down on her low stool and sang to the beast as she milked her. Mary's bucket was full to the brim: there would be plenty for Pat and the children today. She thanked the cow, and said a prayer of thanks to her sweet holy Mary and Jesus for sending the beast.

The cow wandered on to the next house and they milked her too, and got another pail full of milk. That cow kept wandering on all day, and at each house it was the same story. She must have been milked ten times a day, and everyone got a bucketful of milk from her. She was a most generous beast and had the sweetest nature.

The cow stayed for about a week in the Querrin district and then moved on to another place. She wandered all over west Clare, and wherever she went the people were glad to see the generous cow, and thanked God for her visit.

There was one man, however, who thought he would shut the cow in a cabin to stop her wandering, so he could keep all the milk to feed his own family. He put her into a little stone hut and closed the door, putting heavy stones outside it, in case she kicked against it. When he woke next morning the stones were missing, the cabin door was open and the cow was gone and she never came back to his house.

When the famine was over, and food was plentiful again, the cow just stopped coming round the houses. No one knew where she had come from, or where she went, but all were grateful.

MICKIE DEVANEY'S TERRIER

There was a man named Mickie Devaney who had a dog that he loved and adored. It was an Irish Terrier by breed. That is one of those big dogs, with a beard and moustache like the ancient Celtic warriors, and big bushy eyebrows. Mickie just loved that dog, and he had trained it well. He used to let the dog sleep in the room by the fire at night.

Mickie lived in a small cottage with just the two rooms: one where the fire was kept going all day long and another where Mickie had his bed.

Before going to his bed, Mickie would rake up the fire so it would be easy to get it going again in the morning. Then he'd fill the kettle with water and hang it on the hook. He'd say goodnight to the dog and watch him do his three circuits round the mat by the fire before he'd settle himself down for the night. Then Mickie would go through into his bedroom and settle himself down for a good night's peaceful sleep. Mickie always slept like a log after his day's honest toil, and nothing would disturb him until the morning.

Mickie didn't have an alarm clock in the house, for he had no need of one. You will remember, he had the dog trained well. At seven o'clock every morning, the dog would get

up and scratch out the ashes in the grate. You know how it was with the turf fire, it would just get going again as soon as there was a bit of air around it. The dog would drop a couple of turfs onto the fire from the basket. Once the fire was going, the kettle that Mickie had filled the night before would be warming up nicely. When the kettle came to the boil, the dog would jump up on Mickie's bed, lick his face for his morning wash, and bark in his ear to let him know the water was ready for his tea. He was a great dog altogether. You couldn't help but love a dog like that.

However, a neighbour's dog took exception to Mickie Devaney's terrier. Whenever Mickie and his dog were out walking near the boundary with that neighbour's fields, this dog would come throwing itself against the fence, barking ferociously with his hackles raised and his teeth bared, ready for a fight. Now Mickie Devaney's terrier was no angel. For all he was a most intelligent creature, he was after all a dog and he did what dogs do. When the neighbour's dog came running, he would bare his teeth, raise his own hackles, and bark every bit as loud and fiercely as the other dog. There was no love lost between them. If the two could have reached each other they'd have had their teeth in each other's throats in no time.

After many years of loyal companionship, one sad day, Mickie Devaney's beloved terrier died. Can you just imagine it? The poor man was distraught at the loss of such a faithful old friend and servant. So, did he bury the creature under an apple tree so he'd have something to remember him by? Not at all. Mickie Devaney loved that dog so much he got the creature skinned and had his pelt made into a waistcoat. Then he could wear his old friend close to his heart every day.

It wasn't long after that when Mickie was walking by that neighbour's field one night, wearing the dog-skin waistcoat. The neighbour's dog came throwing itself against the fence, just as it always did when Mickie's dog was with him. It must have caught the scent still fresh from the waistcoat. That neighbour's dog was barking and baring its teeth just like before, with its hackles raised. And do you know what happened? The hairs on Mickie's waistcoat stood straight up, preparing for a fight, just as if Mickie's own dog was still present!

THE WEASEL'S CURE

There is an old country belief that if you see a weasel when you are out walking, you should raise your hat and greet it and treat it with the utmost courtesy.

There was a man named Mikey living in the village of Loughisle, near Scarriff, who saw a strange sight as he was walking to his work one morning.

He saw a rat and a weasel together in a struggle to the death. Remembering to treat the weasel with courtesy, Mikey put his boot on the rat's back so that the weasel could escape. The weasel looked up at him gratefully, and quickly ran off. But the rat turned its head around and bit Mikey on his ankle just above the top of his boot. Mikey stepped off the rat and it too ran off.

Now, although the rat's bite is not a terribly big wound, you never know where the rat has been. After a few days the bite on Mikey's ankle turned septic. Soon Mikey's whole leg was red and swollen and he had a fever that gave him chills and sweats at all hours of the day and night. Poor Mikey was at death's door. It went on like that for several days and nights. Mikey would toss and turn, and mumble strange words. Every now and then he would sit up and shout something unintelligible, and fall back into his fevered sleep.

Every morning, while Mikey lay in bed with the fever, the weasel came to his front door and sat there for a while, then went off on its way.

There was a travelling woman called Mrs Scott came by Mikey's house one day. When she heard the news of Mikey's fever and how he had come by it, she asked, 'Is there some creature comes to the house each day? Anything behaving strangely?'

Mikey's wife said, 'Well, there is a weasel been coming to sit on the doorstep every morning since Mikey got sick. Why do you want to know? What's that got to do with anything?'

'If I was you, I'd keep an eye on that weasel. Watch out for it tomorrow morning. See if it brings anything with it.

If it brings something, then put that on the wound. It could be the weasel is trying to help Mikey, just as he helped it.'

Mikey's wife didn't know what to think. It sounded like superstitious nonsense, the very idea of it! But then, nothing else had helped Mikey so far, so maybe it would be worth a try? So next morning she was up and watching for the weasel. Sure enough, the creature brought a leaf off a briar bush in its mouth, and left it on the doorstep.

Mikey's wife took the briar leaf and put it on the wound, binding it there with a bandage.

It wasn't long before the swelling in Mikey's leg began to subside. The colour changed from red to something more ordinary and the wound started to heal. The fever passed and Mikey started to eat again, and soon was good as ever he'd been. His strength returned and he went back to his normal everyday work.

Ever since that time, everyone in Loughisle remembers never to mistreat a weasel. They say it is unlucky. So, if you should meet a weasel when you are out walking, raise your hat to it and greet it politely.

One man, however, forgot this piece of advice, and had a run in with a weasel that taught him a thing or two. He was bachelor who kept a number of geese and ducks around the place. There was no trouble there at all, until in one unfortunate night he lost ten ducks and two of his geese. He wondered if it was a fox, but soon he discovered the cause of his losses was a weasel. The man determined that he would put an end to that scoundrel, and went out searching for the weasel's nest. When he found it, there was six kits in there, as well as the two adults. He was so angry, he had no mercy for them after what they had done to his birds, so he killed them all, except one of the fully-grown weasels, which ran off and escaped.

When he got back home the man made himself a pot of tea and sat down in his comfortable chair, feeling justifiably avenged. He was about to put some milk he had in a jar in his tea, when a weasel came right up onto his table up and spat in the milk jar. It was the one that had escaped his revenge.

The man belated remembered the danger of crossing a weasel and knew what he had to do. He went back and tried to make good the damage he'd done to the weasel's nest. He did the best he could and when he got home again, there was the weasel waiting for him by his chair. The creature came up on the table then and spilled some of the milk from the jar onto the ground. Then it covered it over with dust and dirt. The weasel looked the man in the eye, then looked back at the spilt milk and shook its head. The man knew the weasel was telling him not to drink the spoiled milk.

After that the man and the weasel had a kind of understanding between them. Neither one did any harm to the other. No more geese or ducks were taken. No more kits destroyed. Every day the weasel came into the house and the man gave it food and milk from his own table. At first they just respected each other, and kept a bit of distance, but as time went on they became good companions. When the weasel died, at a great age for a weasel, it was in the arms of his old friend that he took his last breath.

THE RAT CHARMER OF FEAKLE

There must have been a lot of rats about in the old days, for there was a whole profession known as rat charming. Croohore Tadg was a well-known rat charmer who lived in the parish of Feakle. He had a black dog, and wherever the man went, the dog was always in his company. It was a huge beast, the size of a calf, and had eyes that shone red like fire. People said it was enchanted, and were scared if they saw it at night.

Now, Crohoore Tadg had a fearsome reputation: he could kill you or cure you if he liked. All he had to do was say the word and the rats would leave and go wherever he told them to. That was rat-charming for you. The rats would do whatever the charmer told them to. Whether they wanted to or not just didn't come into it. I can't say that he was a popular fellow. He was probably feared by people because of his strange power over the creatures, but he was obviously needed at times.

He didn't mind who he worked for or where he sent the rats. If one neighbour fell out with another and wished him ill luck, he could pay Croohore Tadg to send all the rats from his place to his neighbour's. All the rats would turn up at the neighbour's place like a plague of rats, scuttling in under the barn door, into the house. When he did this, the rat at the front of the pack would have a message for the neighbour. There would be a note in its mouth or tied with a bit of string around its neck. Tadg wrote the note himself, saying that if they had a problem with rats they could contact him: he was the man to rid you of rats. The note said where they could find him and how much it would cost. It was just like leaving a business card advertising his services.

One day, a publican refused to serve Crohoore Tadg a pint of porter. The rat charmer took offense at this and sent a big pack of rats to the publican's house. He told the rats to eat and drink whatever they found there. You know as well as I do the damage that one rat can do, let alone a whole pack of them. The unfortunate publican had to send for

Crohoore Tadg and make an apology to him. He said he'd pay him well if he'd take the rats away. That was how he operated, so you can see he wasn't a popular man.

He could be very cruel too. One day a rat chewed a hole in Croohore Tadg's boot. Well, a good pair of boots cost a lot in those days, and he was mad with that rat then. He took his razor and fastened it to a piece of turf. He spoke to the rat and told it to go and cut its throat on the razor. The rat went up to the razor and sat there on its back legs, squealing and turning its face away. It didn't want to go any further. But when Tadg told it again, it had to do it – it had to cut itself on the razor.

The parish priest was no friend of Croohore Tadg. He thought he had no right using magical power to interfere with creatures, or to help others wish ill on their neighbours. One day they had a contest between them to see who was more powerful, the priest or the rat charmer. They were out in the field and the priest saw two black crows sitting on a branch of a tree. The priest said, 'We will take one of these crows each, and see which of us can get them down first.'

'I will beat you for sure,' said Croohore Tadg. 'I'll have mine down and plucked before you have even started!'

The charmer won the contest and the priest was mad with him. They fought against each other with words rather than blows, till the priest shouted at him 'Croohore Tadg, you will be buried alive one day!' The priest spat the words out like a curse, which is not quite what he had intended, but he was so angry he could not help himself.

Tadg replied with a laugh and a curse of his own, 'Hah! You would die even if I was never born, but if the stones of the chapel should fall on you and lie there like a tombstone, then it is myself that wished it there!'

Not so long after that, a storm blew up and the wind shook the trees around the chapel. Suddenly a heavy branch broke and fell on the gable wall. A large stone fell loose, and hit the priest on the head. The people looked on in shock and amazement, as the priest was crushed under the big stone. It was too heavy for anyone to move it, so it lay on top of the priest like a tombstone until four strong men arrived to move it, so the man could be given a decent burial.

A while after that, Tadg was at a wedding at Derrynagitta. The house was packed with neighbours, friends and relations of the happy couple. People were eating and drinking. The women were back and forth with plates and glasses, but Croohore Tadg was there a good long time before anyone offered him a drink. He was fed up with the wait and got up from his seat in the corner, ready to leave for home, saying, 'I always heard Derrynagitta was a wet place, but it is mighty dry here tonight!'

When they heard him, the women brought him a jug of whiskey, and bade him sit back down and enjoy his drink. He stayed and drank his fill, and he didn't leave until late in the night. It was a dark night and he fell in a ditch when he was walking home. When the people found him next day, they thought he was dead. They fetched a coffin and put him in it, and put the lid on the coffin. Later a boy heard scratching inside the coffin and he thought it was a rat shut in the coffin with the rat charmer.

The truth was that Croohore Tadg wasn't dead at all. But they did not get him out of the coffin. They were glad to be rid of him.

After Croohore Tadg died, they could not find his black dog anywhere, but people said it was still seen sometimes after dark, on the roads around Feakle, Tulla and Drumcharley.

References:

White Horses by the Shannon Shore: SFS (1937-38) Arthur McGuire, Cross, told to Patrick MaGuire, Kilkee.

The Sea Horse: SFS (1937-38) Norah Howe, told by Patrick Crowe, Caherduff, Dunsallagh NS, p.230.

MacNamara's Foal: SFS (1937-38) Patrick Benson, Kilkishen, p.348.

The Three Cows Come to Ireland: Concerning Cows, in *Ancient Legends, Mystic Charms, And Sperstitions of Ireland*, Lady Jane Wilde (Chatto & Windus; London, 1919); SFS, Michael Rynne, told to Patrick McNulty, Cahereskin, Ennistymon.

A Plentiful Cow: SFS (1937-38) no name.

Mickey Devaney's Terrier: SFS (1937-38) James MacNamara, Ballylickey, Quin told to Eilish MacNamara, An Daingan School, p.3.

The Weasel's Cure: SFS (1937-38) Patrick Dillon, Loughisle, Scariff, An Capach Ban, Moynoe, p.178.

The Rat Charmer of Feakle: Heard around Tulla and Feakle many years ago.

11

MONSTERS

THE MONSTER OF CULLAUN LAKE

Between Kilkishen and Tulla lies a beautiful lake called
Cullaun Lake that has a reputation for being enchanted.

A man called Pat Murphy had land that stretched down
to the lake's edge. He decided to set aside a bit of it for
meadowing, so he fenced it off to keep his cattle from
that field. Pat noticed a strange thing: the grass in his field
was never as lush and green as he expected it should be.
He suspected his neighbours of putting their beasts in to
graze his field at night and taking them away early in the
morning. He decided to stay up one night to see if he could
catch them at it.

The night was quiet and lit by a large silver moon. Pat
concealed himself behind some rocks and bushes to wait.
At the stroke of midnight, a dark cloud came and covered
the moon. A shiver ran down Pat's spine as he heard the
stillness of the night broken by the shrieking of gulls and

a strange, dull crunching sound. How Pat wished he had stayed warm and safe in his bed, but now he was paralysed with fear, and could not run away if he tried. He trembled under the bushes that suddenly seemed a very poor protection from whatever was coming towards him.

The crunching sound grew closer and closer. A breeze blew the dark cloud from the face of the moon, making it light enough for Pat to catch a glimpse what was making the sound. What he saw nearly caused Pat's heart to stop and he clung in terror to the bushes. Whatever it was, it seemed a huge creature, like a monstrous eel or water snake, that crawled on its belly over the field. As it drew itself over the ground, it consumed vast swathes of grass with a hideous crunching sound.

His face ashen and his eyes wild with fear, Pat waited the long cold hours until daybreak, when the monster, having finally eaten its fill, coiled its vast body around in a circle and made its way back to the lake. With the light of the sun, Pat's courage returned. He crawled out from under his bush and shook himself to warm his blood. He stood up then to make sure to get a good look at the monster. What he saw had the appearance of a gigantic eel, over ten feet long and with a ferocious frill of a mane along its back.

As the creature slid back into the lake, the waters bubbled as if its surface was a pot of water on the boil. Giant waves rolled over the shore, leaving a ragged trail of leaves and branches in their wake. The air was darkened by the sudden flight of birds disturbed from where they slept, all shrieking with fright. Pat covered his ears against their wailing, and out of his own throat came a cry of awful torment and terror. Exhausted after this final fearsome sight, Pat fell down on the ground, quite still and totally unconscious, his mouth still open in contorted the shape of his scream.

Hours later his neighbours found him crawling along the edge of the lake on his hands and knees, only half conscious, mumbling incoherently to himself. They brought him home and put him in his bed, but when they asked him what had happened that had frightened him so, he was unable to speak more than a couple of stumblingly incoherent words, 'Mo, mo, monster ... li, like an eel ...'

Pat remained in his bed from that day, and was not able to do a day's work after that.

THE BROC SIDHE OF RATH

Between Lahinch and Liscannor there is an old church called Kilmacreehy. It was named after St MacCreehy, who founded a school there in the sixth century. But perhaps MacCreehy's main claim to fame was for banishing the fairy badger. 'The what?' you may be wondering, but yes, you did read it right, the fairy badger. It was known as the Broc Sidhe, or Bruckee, of Rath. This creature, which some people think might have been a bear, lived in a cave called Poulnabruckee, near Rath Lake, at the foot of Scumhall.

Rath Lake is just a small lake and its edges are marshy and covered with reeds. The demon badger used to round up any cattle grazing nearby and drive them into the lake where he would devour them. The Bruckee had a huge appetite, and the people around Scumhall didn't know what to do about it.

It was taking large numbers of their cattle every year and so they pleaded with the saints to come to their aid. The saints came, four or five, one after another, and prayed, holding up their staffs and commanding the beast to go back to its cave and never to return, but all to no avail. Still the Bruckee advanced with its ferocious jaws opened wide, showing its sharp teeth.

St Blathmac came and tackled the beast with his bell and his staff and his wits. It was a long hard battle and the creature grew ever more fearsome but the saint refused to give up. Just as it seemed that he would lose the day, St Macreehy came along to add his strength to the fight. MacCreehy had already proved himself by slaying a gigantic eel that rose from the waters of Liscannor Bay and ravaged the graves of the dead in the old churchyard there.

MacCreehy faced the Bruckee fearlessly, and eventually he got the upper hand. He cornered the monster in its cave, bound it in chains and cast it to the bottom of the lake, but he gave it permission to rise to the surface once every seven years.

Even as late as the 1930s, the creature was seen very early in the morning by two men who were out fishing. By this time, the creature seemed to have learnt the art of changing its shape and appearance, and it did this every hour or so. When you'd just got used to seeing it as a horse and a harrow, it quickly changed itself into the guise of a rick of turf! After that it took on the shape of a house. All day long it kept changing its shape. At nightfall it disappeared into the lake again, and it hasn't been seen again since. But then again, no one has really been looking for it.

The people remembered the brave St MacCreehy, the Bruckee-slayer, and a carving of the Bruckee is still there on a stone in the old church at Kilmacreehy.

THE BOAR THE CAT AND THE SERPENT

There were, at one time, three monsters that terrorised the people in the area around Doolough Lake and Mount Callan.

The first was an enormous wild cat that had made its home at Craig na Seanean, by a small stream whose waters ran into a river that eventually reached Doolough Lake. It used to kill fowl and lambs, and even young calves. Everyone lived in fear of this cat because of its tail, which was over seven feet long and had three claws in its tip. The cat would swing its tail like a whip, tearing at the flesh of whoever was unlucky enough to come within its range. It was a terror to the neighbourhood, and although the people tried to kill it, it always seemed to come back.

Another of these monsters was a particularly huge wild boar, or turc, that roamed the district to the east of Doolough Lake. The boar stood over seven feet tall and bore two lengthy tusks sharp as spears. That beast caused enormous devastation, crashing through walls and fences, flattening trees, hurling boulders and tearing up the land with its heavy feet. It was even more terrifying than the wild cat, causing harm to cattle and to the people themselves.

As if that were not enough, it was around this same time that St Senan famously defeated the Catach and banished it to Doolough Lake on Mount Callan (and as this story is told elsewhere, I won't tell it to you now), where it was condemned to live on an eel. The Catach was a ferocious sea serpent over 3 miles long that used to inhabit the waters around Inis Cathaigh (Scattery Island) in the Shannon. They say it could circle around Inis Cathaigh and put its tail in its mouth. It used to cause boats to capsize and many lives were lost in the deep waters. Although the good saint had secured the monster with a chain and commanded it to do no further harm, the Catach was still seen on dark days in that dark and gloomy lough. The people were afraid it might break its chain, and no one knew what destruction it would wreak in the area if it had its freedom.

Ah yes, these were dangerous times, but they were also times when young men were hungry for heroic challenges and adventures.

Around this same time, far in the north, the wife of the King of Ulster died, leaving her three sons without a mother to love and care for them. The king was heartbroken, for he had loved his wife dearly, but being realistic he knew he must marry again for the sake of his children. The woman he took as his new wife proved to be cruel, wicked and vain. Marry in haste, repent at leisure. Perhaps if he had waited a little while he might have made a wiser choice, but such are the benefits of hindsight. The new queen had no wish to look after her new husband's three sons. In fact, she'd rather they were sent far away, the further the better. She played a game of cards with them, with forfeits for the losers. The two older sons lost to her. The forfeit she demanded of the first two sons was that they should go to County Clare on a challenging quest. The challenge was that they must hunt and kill the wild boar of Mount Callan, the wild cat of Craig na Seanean and the Catach of Doolough Lake. These challenges were far enough away, and dangerous enough that they would be well out of her way, and indeed, if she was lucky, they might not ever return. The youngest son won his game against her and he demanded, as forfeit, that his stepmother be incarcerated in the highest tower in his father's palace on bread and water until he and his brothers returned from their adventures.

The three young men set off early the next day on horseback, and it took them a good two weeks to reach County Clare. They left their horses at Connolly and continued on to Mount Callan on foot. Each of them carried three long spears and a sword. First they sought out the boar, or rather, they had not gone too far before the boar found them. They were just beginning to climb the hill when the boar came crashing towards them, dislodging big rocks and hurling them at the brothers. Dodging the flying boulders, the brothers threw their spears at the angry beast, but its hide was so thick the spears just bounced off. They were not to be put off, but pursued the beast all day. Just before nightfall they found the boar in his cave, enjoying the spoils of his day's foraging. They goaded and teased him with their spears until he came out of the safety of his cave and then the battle began. The brothers used their weapons as best they could. The boar used its bulk and its long tusks against them, wounding one of the brothers. The light was fading, but at last, with their swords upright they struck the boar in the neck and killed him. They cleaned their brother's wound, saw that it was not too deep, and being young and strong he soon recovered. They cut off the boar's head and put the trophy on a rock. That gave the name to that place, Cean Turc, that is now Connolly.

The following day they sought out the wild cat. They found it by the stream, and had another battle. It took four

hours of heavy fighting, the cat employing its long and clawed tail to make sure the brothers kept their distance. One of the brothers sliced off the ferocious tail with his sword, and after that the cat presented little further challenge.

Having beaten the boar and the cat, the triumphant brothers went on to Doolough Lake to tackle the serpent. The Catach was fastened with a chain and could not leave the lake. Though it coiled and spat at them, showing its sharp teeth, it could not harm the brothers, because of St Senan's spell. When they sliced through its long neck, the sea serpent's blood spilled into the water and over the land around them. Where the Catach's blood touched the ground the grass that grows there stays bright and lush, whether it is winter or summer.

Now the three young Ulster princes had defeated all three monsters; they had fulfilled their forfeits to their stepmother and could return home.

I do not know the story of their journey home, but I do know that if I was one of them, I would be in no rush to release the new queen from her prison in the palace tower. I wonder if their adventures in County Clare whetted their appetite for adventure, so perhaps they went on to further quests, and took the long road home.

References:

The Monster of Cullaun Lake: SFS (1937-38) From old people in Quin, Ballycar, p.232; I also heard this story whilst walking at Cullaun Lake.

The Broc Sidhe of Rath: SFS (1937-38) Patrick McGuane, Scumhall, Corofin, heard from his father, Diseart, p. 43.

The Boar, the Cat and the Serpent: SFS (1937-38) Maire ni Concubair, Kilmihil, Cahermurphy School, p.131.

12

JOKERS &
TRICKSTERS

I remember hearing this next story long ago, in a cottage near Tulla. My friends' old neighbour was in their kitchen, sitting in the corner by the range in his finest suit and hat, supping a cup of extra-strong tea. His trousers were too loose for him at the waist and he had fashioned a belt for himself with some brightly coloured baler twine. His dark eyes twinkled in the poor light, as he told tales of young fellows' devilment.

A SOBERING THOUGHT

There was an old bachelor who lived somewhere between Tulla and Ennis who loved nothing more than to go eating and drinking the town of Ennis. This man had a great appetite, and he mightily enjoyed his food, so whatever you had served him up, he would be thanking you after it as if it were the best of *cordon bleu* cooking, even though it were just bacon and cabbage. And when he'd eaten his fill of it, he enjoyed his pint or two of porter, and whatever you're having yourself.

Every Saturday he made his way to Ennis on his ass and car. He'd be there all day, meeting his old cronies and talking about the price of this and the cost of that, and wheeling and dealing and eating and drinking. By the time he was back on his ass and car and ready for the journey home, it was dark already. He was that fond of the drink that he usually had more than was good for him. Sometimes he'd be singing loudly along the road, but just as often he would fall asleep on the car. Well now, the ass had walked that road so often, it knew the way and could bring him home without him needing to direct it.

So this one night he'd had more than enough to drink, and he was fast asleep on the car all the way from Ennis. He was so drunk that he didn't wake when the ass had stopped outside the gate. He just slept there, where he was.

Now, there were four lads passing that night that knew him well, and they found him snoring away fast asleep on the car outside his own gate. The lads thought they would have some sport with old fellow, and play a trick on him.

They lifted him down from the car and carried him into his own house, and were careful not to laugh out loud in case they woke him. Then they unhitched the ass from the car and brought the ass inside the house too.

Next they took the wheels off the car and carried it into the house. When they'd got all that inside, they brought in the wheels and put them back under the car again. The lads hitched the ass to the car again, and gently lifted the old fellow back up onto the car, and all this time the old man is still snoring away, fast asleep.

When they had that all done, the lads went out and closed the door behind them. Oh, they laughed all the way home at what they'd done, wondering what the old fellow would make of it when he woke up on the cart inside the house.

Well, when the man awoke, he could not believe his eyes! He nearly died of fright when he saw he was on the ass car – in his own kitchen! He sat there rubbing his eyes, shaking his head, trying to make sense of it all. He knew there was no way the ass and car would pass through the door of the house. It was just too wide! He thought it must have been the fairies playing tricks on him. Or maybe he did have too much to drink last night? This last thought was a sobering one for the old bachelor, and he never came home drunk from the town of Ennis again.

THE BIGGEST FOOL

There were three women who were neighbours out in the country somewhere. Each of them was called Mary, and each of them was married to a man called John.

Christmas was coming soon, and it was time for the three Marys to go to the nearest town to bring home the Christmas. They were clever women who knew the price of shoe leather, so they wore their best dresses and walked barefooted, carrying their shoes and stockings in their hands. They would put on their shoes and stockings to look respectable when they reached the edge of the town. On their backs they were carrying big baskets full of eggs and butter to sell, and they were sure to get plenty of money to enjoy their day in the town.

They had a great day, sold all the eggs and butter, and bought in everything they would need for the Christmas feast.

They were talking over the events of the day as they walked homewards, when they spotted a large brown paper parcel all tied up with striped string sitting in the middle of the road ahead of them. They agreed that the first to reach the parcel could claim it as her own. They began to run, each trying to be first to touch it. All three reached it at the same moment, and they began to quarrel about who had the most right to open the package.

A man was coming along the road just then and saw the women quarrelling. He stopped and asked what they were fighting about. The women explained the situation, and they asked if he could decide the matter for them.

He paused to think for a moment and then he said, 'My dear ladies, I believe I have found the solution to your conundrum.' He was obviously a learned man. 'Let me take charge of the parcel for now. The winner should be the one of you that makes the biggest fool of her husband once you get home. I cannot say fairer than that.'

The women agreed, and they went on their way. They reached home just as the sun was setting.

When the first Mary got home, her husband said to her, 'Did you have a grand day at the town?' Mary did not answer him, but just got on with her work. John did not know what the matter with her was. Had he done something to anger her? He went out for a bit, thinking that would give her time to cool off. When he came back in, he asked her if she had the tea ready. 'Why would I be giving a strange man tea, when my own husband is out working in the haggard? Go out and call him in.' John did as his wife said, and out he went to the haggard, but of course there was no man out there. So that was how the first John was fooled.

The second Mary, when she got home, told her husband John that he was dead. He did not believe her at first, but as his wife just kept on telling him so, in the end he had to believe her, it must be so. Mary sent for the coffin and held the wake and arranged the funeral for the following day. So that was how the second John was fooled.

The third Mary, she stayed at the wake that night and went home early the next morning. She found her husband still asleep in his bed. She shook him awake, saying, 'Why are ye in your bed? Did ye not think to go to the funeral with all your neighbours?'

'I never heard of a funeral,' said the third John. 'Who is it that died?'

'It was your good neighbour John that died.' said Mary. 'They are just leaving the house now. If you are quick you can join them.'

John leapt for his clothes, but Mary said, 'You've no time for putting on clothes. You best run along as you are, or you will be too late!'

So John ran out as he was, after the funeral. When the people saw the naked man running towards them, they thought he must be mad, and possibly dangerous! The men carrying the coffin set it down on the road and the people ran off in all directions.

When John got to the coffin, he took off the lid, and there he found his good friend, not dead at all, but wondering what was John doing naked at his funeral? When they realised how they had been fooled by their wives, the men laughed out loud and made their way back home.

So that was how the three Marys fooled their husbands. Now, which one of the women do you think got the parcel?

A FINE GENTLEMAN

There was once a blacksmith by the name O'Connor who
lived at Mount Callan. He worked hard at his trade and
had a reputation for quality and reliability. If he said he
would do something for you, you knew that he would do
it. The blacksmith was married and he had one son, who
was now a grown man. I suppose he expected the son to
follow him in his trade and become a blacksmith, but
the son was a disappointment to him, as he never did a
day's work, not in the forge nor anywhere else. He would
wander the roads doing nothing, just seeing where the
road would take him, blackguarding his way through life.
He was a cheat and a liar, and would sell his own father if
he could find a buyer! O'Connor thought it such a waste
that his son was a wastrel, but what could he do about
that now?

There was an English gentleman travelling in the west of
Ireland. One day he came to Spanish Point to take the air,
and there he met the young O'Connor and thought him a
charming fellow, with great wit, and with terribly amusing
stories to tell. The gentleman decided to bring him back
to England with him. The young man agreed, and they
travelled over the sea.

When they arrived in England, the gentleman paid a
tailor to measure the young O'Connor and make him a suit
of smart clothes in a fine wool cloth with a narrow stripe,
with a waistcoat and a silk cravat. He bought him a gold
watch on a chain to fit in the waistcoat pocket. He bought
him a good set of boots of shining black leather, and a tall
stovepipe hat. What a transformation: the young O'Connor
looked every inch a gentleman, quite handsome, and well-
dressed in the fashionable clothes of the day.

When the gentleman went visiting a friend he brought O'Connor with him. The door of the house was opened by a servant who bowed low before them and showed them into a parlour. Here men and women sat on plump brocade sofas and chairs with gilded legs, sharing polite conversation and enjoying small cakes and fancies from china plates. The gentleman presented the young man to the company as 'The son of Lord O'Connor of Mount Callan, whose acquaintance I was pleased to make whilst on my travels in the land of Ireland'.

The young lady of the house was quite taken by the charming young Irishman, who surely thought he had died and gone to heaven. As she was of a marriageable age, a match was made between the two. Her father sent his trusted steward to Ireland to visit Mount Callan and see what wealth and style she would be marrying into.

When he reached Ennis, the steward enquired for directions to Lord O'Connor's of Mount Callan's estate. People were puzzled, and no one he asked could tell him where this was. At last an old woman told him, 'I never heard of a Lord O'Connor, but there is a little blacksmith by name of O'Connor who lives at Mount Callan. Maybe he'd be the one you are looking for?'

The steward set off for Mount Callan to see what he would find there. As he came to the forge, he met with seven goats in the doorway. The blacksmith was eating his dinner, and what a sight he was, sitting on the side of an old pig in the corner and eating potatoes with his hands out of an old scuttle! When he had finished eating, he got up off the pig, washed his greasy hands in a bog of water, dried them on his apron and reached out to shake the visitor's hand.

The steward asked if he had by any chance a son. 'Oh, I do indeed,' said the blacksmith. 'And is he not the biggest wastrel and blackguard that ever there was? He is gone these last months and I do not know where, and a shame to his father he is that never did a day's work for his keep.'

The steward set off back to England, wondering what he would say to his master about what he had seen. The Lord O'Connor's estate was just a humble pigsty of a place! There was obviously no money, no land, and no manners. Before he reached his master's house, the gentleman met him on the road, saying, 'I will give you ten good English pounds if you will paint your master a pretty picture of Lord O'Connor and his estate.'

'I do not wish to lie to my master, sir.' said the steward. 'He knows me to be an honest man.'

'Ah, I see, but could you stretch the truth a little? This ten pounds is yours if you can.'

The steward smiled as he tucked the money inside his shirt and went straight home.

They all came out to meet him, the master and his daughter, the prospective bride, and all their fancy guests dressed in their finest clothes. 'Well, man, what was it like? Tell us all about the Lord O'Connor and his estate in the west of Ireland.'

The steward took a deep breath and prepared to stretch the truth of what he had seen, without actually telling a lie. 'When I reached Lord O'Connor's abode, I was saluted at the entrance by seven upstanding guards. Their master was eating his dinner when I arrived, and I waited until he had finished before I approached him. He was sat upon a most handsome and generously upholstered chair, eating from a platter with cutlery the like of which you would rarely see in England. He washed before he shook my hand, and the vessel in which he washed, well, all the money in England could not buy the like. The fine cloth on which he dried himself, could not be compared with any woven in England.'

'You need say no more, steward,' said the master. 'I have heard enough to know that my daughter is marrying into a fine family. Let the wedding take place tonight!'

And so it was, the two were married, and lived happily in England thereafter, never visiting the 'estate of Lord O'Connor', which perhaps was for the best, after all.

References:

The Biggest Fool: SFS (1937-38) Sean O Griobia, Glean Mor, Kilmihil, Clonigulane School.

A Fine Gentleman: SFS (1937-38) Michael MacDonnell, Carhunagry, Mullagh told to Mary O'Gorman, Carhunagry, Mullagh, County Clare, p.259.

GLOSSARY

Ass and car: Donkey and cart

Boreen/bohereen: A small road, track

Leaba: Bed

Lios: Ring fort

Geasa: An obligation

Spancil: A rope used to hobble an animal, especially a horse or cow

Firkin: A measure of butter, somewhere around 25kg

Tuatha De Danaan: People of the goddess Danu, a particularly gifted race, with powers to influence the elements; one of a series of races who settled in Ireland. When the Milesians came, the Tuatha De Danaans agreed to settle within the hollow hills, and later shrank in the people's imaginations to become the 'Little People' or the Sidhe.

PRONUNCIATION GUIDE

For the benefit for non-Irish speakers (like me), here is a rough guide to some of the trickier looking names and words.

Irish	Pronounced
Aithirné	ath-ir-na
Aoibheall	ee-vul
Bo Dubh	bo duv
Cailleach	kal-yach
Caoilte	keel-cha or kweel-cha
Catach	catach (ch as in loch)
Ceannir	kee-an-eer
Croohore Tadg	krow hoar tyg
Diarmid	jeer-mid or deer-mid
Eochaidh	yeo-hee
Feakle	feek-al
Fiachra	feea-kra
Fionn Mac Cumhall	fin mac kool
Geasa	gees-ah
Glas Gaibreac	gloss guy-brach

Goban Saor	gubbawn seer
Gaba Ruad	goweru
Grian	gree-an
Grainne	grawn-ya
Inis Cataigh	inish katah
Leaba na Glaise	labba na glash
Lough Derg Dheirc	loch derg jerrik
Mac Tail	mac tawll
Maire Ruad	maw-ra roo-a
Ruaidhin	roo-ay-een
Scriobhan	scree von
Sidhe	shee
Sliabh na Glaise	sleev na glass
Stuiffeen	stuff-een